LESS[illegible] LOVE

A LONELY HE[illegible] BOOK CLUB NOVEL

HANNAH LYNN

PAPER CAT PUBLISHING

ALSO BY HANNAH LYNN

Standalone Feel Good Novels

The Afterlife of Walter Augustus

In at the Deep End

The Side Hustle

The Complete Peas and Carrots Series

Peas, Carrots and an Aston Martin

Peas, Carrots and a Red Feather Boa

Peas, Carrots and Six More Feet

Peas, Carrots and Lessons in Life

Peas, Carrots and Panic at the Plot

Peas, Carrots and Happily Ever After

The Holly Berry Sweet Shop Series

The Sweet Shop of Second Chances

Love Blooms at the Second Chances Sweet Shop

Family Ties at the Second Chances Sweet Shop

High Hopes at the Second Chances Sweet Shop

Sunday Days at the Second Chances Sweet Shop

A Summer Wedding at the Second Chances Sweet Shop

Snowflakes over the Second Chances Sweet Shop

The Complete Lonely Hearts Book Club Series

Never Too Late

Lessons in Love

Illusions of Love

Table for Two

Dishing up Romance

The Complete Wildflower Lock Series

New Beginnings at Wildflower Lock

Coffee and Cake at Wildflower Lock

Blue Skies Over Wildflower Lock

Forever Love at Wildflower Lock

This story is a work of fiction. All names, characters, organisations, places, events and incidents are products of the author's imagination or are used fictitiously. Any resemblance to any persons, alive or dead or events is entirely coincidental.

First published 2023

Published by Paper Cat Publishing

ISBN: 978-1-915346-16-2

Cover by Diane Meacham
Edited by Eleanor Lease

To Claire, who brought us all together,

CHAPTER 1

Jules stared at her computer screen, wondering where to start. It made no sense how quickly the last six weeks had gone. It felt like only yesterday that she'd been saying goodbye to her old class, hugging her colleagues, and trying not to look too envious as they talked about all the trips they had planned over the long summer break. Her teaching assistant was inter-railing around Europe with her mother, while the assistant head had taken it one step further and accepted a post in Venezuela. Jules, however, had stayed in Maldon. She always stayed in Maldon. Not that she minded much.

Six weeks had felt like more than enough time to really relax, recuperate and spend some quality time with Austin before he took the leap into secondary school. Her baby boy, all grown up. If she thought about it too much, she knew she'd end up crying, not out of sadness, but shock. And so, they had made it a rule that they would not mention secondary school until the very last week of the holidays. Fortunately, there was plenty to keep them busy during the summer in Maldon.

The small Essex town was picture perfect, and never more so than during those mid-year months, when the river would fill with sailboats, which bobbed lazily in the wind. While all along the seawall, families enjoyed the sun, eating ice creams and chips, while dodging the seagulls, who assumed that half the portion was for them.

This summer had been no different. Jules and Austin had tried to make the most of the perfect weather, with walks along the nearby canals, picnics by the picturesque locks, and cycles down the tow paths. In the fourth week, one of Austin's friends, who had gone to Italy with his family for a fortnight, had lent them an inflatable two-person kayak to use while he was away. Without doubt, it was the most fun the pair had had together in ages.

But now, in the blink of an eye, that time was gone. She was only forty-eight hours away from her first staff meeting of the year and Austin, who only yesterday had been a tiny baby in her arms, was about to start secondary school, and then he would need her even less than he already did.

While covering her mouth to block a yawn, Jules shifted her position, pushing back her shoulders, and resting her fingers above the laptop keys. The list of jobs she needed to address before the staff meeting was making it tough to know where to start, though, she decided, it was probably a good idea to look at her timetable again. No sooner had Jules clicked on the file than the door to the dining room swung open.

"You cannot be working today?" Vicky said.

When Jules had placed an advert on the local Facebook group five years ago, saying that she was in search of someone to rent their spare room, she had been hoping for somebody quiet, professional and good with children. While quiet was not a word that anyone would ever use to describe Vicky, her lodger more than made up for it in other ways.

Austin had been only six when Vicky moved in, but he took to her like he had known her all his life. Within the first week together, they had developed inside jokes and secret handshakes. Everything about Vicky was loud, from her clothes to her music and most of all her laugh, and it had taken a while for Jules to get used to, but now there was no one in the world she trusted more. Vicky was there, with lasagnes in the oven, when Jules had a late-night parent-teacher evening, or to pick Austin up from school when staff meetings overran. She also took on playing chess with him when he had got too good to play his mum anymore. So now, five years later, and Jules thought of Vicky more as a sister than a friend. And just like a sister, she knew exactly how to rub her up the wrong way.

"Of course I'm working," Jules said, looking up from her laptop. "Or at least, I'm trying to. It's the last weekend before I go back to work."

"Exactly. It is the last weekend before you go back to work. You need to enjoy it."

She should have seen the line coming. After a deep breath in, Jules let out a long sigh.

"I need to do some things to make sure I'm ahead before Monday. We've got a new assistant head starting, and I have no idea what they're going to expect of me. I want to make sure I've got all the data and seating plans sorted. Not to mention the intervention and extension work of the children moving up into my class."

"Well, I am appalled by this attitude." Vicky pulled out a dining chair and dropped into it. "In fact, I think it's totally unacceptable. This is the last weekend of your holidays. The last weekend of summer. We need to go out. We need to have fun somewhere. And by *we* I mean *you*. I don't remember the last time you had a proper night out."

"I go out. I was out last night, remember?" Jules closed the page she was looking at; there was no chance she was going to focus while Vicky was still there, and she wasn't showing any signs of leaving yet.

"Your book club does not count as going out," Vicky protested.

"Why not? I was out of the house, socialising with people. And last night it was in the pub, so that counts as going out."

"It doesn't count, because you will never meet someone in a group that is literally called the Lonely Hearts Book Club."

Jules grunted and tapped loudly on the keyboard. Recently, she'd wished she'd never mentioned the book club's nickname to Vicky. It wasn't an official title, it just so happened that everyone who attended, beside one elderly widow, was absolutely hopeless with romance. So, as well as books, they bonded over their shared histories of failed relationships. While it might sound pessimistic to people on the outside, the book club had given Jules some of the best friends she could have hoped for. And the fact that they were all single too meant she didn't have to spend the evenings hearing how their other halves are just like Mr Darcy, or Charlie Lastra.

Previously, Vicky had never had an issue with the name of the club, or the fact that Jules was content to remain single for the rest of her life, but twelve months ago, Vicky had met Oliver, a Scottish estate agent based in Chelmsford. Since then, she had been pushing Jules more and more to go out and meet someone and said the book club was holding her back from doing that. In truth, though, they both knew there was only one thing holding Jules back. Herself.

"I really do not have time to go out," Jules insisted again. "I've got new student data to work through, and I want to check all the old assessments to make sure I've differentiated the tasks properly."

Talking in teacher jargon was usually a good way to make Vicky back off, and yet she remained seated next to Jules and not moving.

"That's what the Inset day on Monday is for. Honestly, this isn't right. You can't spend your last evenings working like this. Besides, I want to go out. And there's music on at the White Horse."

"Music. That sounds late. Music's always on late."

"We don't have to stay for it if you don't want. We can just do dinner, then head home if you prefer."

Jules chuckled inwardly. There was no such thing as *just dinner* with Vicky, and they both knew it. Dinner was always followed by a couple of cocktails, and then dancing, possibly with shots. Five years together had taught Jules that.

Still, she had one final ace up her sleeve.

"Even if I wanted to go out, you know I can't. I haven't got anyone to look after Austin."

She straightened her back, allowing herself a flicker of satisfaction, as she watched Vicky's lips purse and tighten. It was a face she often made when she was about to say something Jules would not like, so Jules cut in before her friend could speak. "I know what you're going to say. He's eleven and other children his age are left while their parents go out for dinner. And I know he's far more sensible than most children his age, and he'd never do anything deliberately silly, but accidents happen even to sensible people. I can't do it. Maybe next year."

It wasn't the first time that Jules had used this argument, and given how it was perfectly valid, she assumed it would be more than enough to make Vicky back off, which is why she was surprised to see her housemate smiling at her.

"Why are you looking like that?" Jules said.

"Me?" Her lodger folded her arms over her chest. "This may surprise you, but I suspected you were going to say that. In fact, I would have guaranteed it. Which is why I've already asked Mrs Horner next door if she'll keep an eye on him."

"You did what?"

Vicky's grin stretched from ear to ear.

"It's fine. She was quite happy to, actually. You know she doesn't even have Netflix, so she loves babysitting. I told her she could watch whatever films she wanted and set her up with her own profile, so I think she's hoping we'll go away for a weekend now."

Jules's head tilted to the side as she took a moment to process what she just heard.

"You're saying you've already arranged a babysitter?"

"I have. And I bumped into your friend Sophie from the book club too, so she's meeting us there at seven."

This was a new level of manipulation, even from Vicky, and Jules couldn't help but be impressed. She could say no to Vicky easily enough, but Sophie, or any of the book club people – well, that would feel like she was letting them down.

"And do I have any choice in this?"

"No. You can try to argue, but you know I'll win eventually, so it's probably best if you just give up now."

Jules offered one last glance at the laptop screen where a to-do list was currently central. Anyone who thought teachers spent all six weeks of their summer holiday in a permanent state of relaxation had obviously never met one outside a classroom. But Vicky was right. This was her last weekend, and there was no chance she'd get out and about once the term began.

"Fine, but we really are just going for dinner.'

CHAPTER 2

The warm summer sun was still hours away from setting and cast long shadows along the road as Jules linked her arms with Vicky and headed towards Maldon high street. This small town, tucked away in the East Essex countryside, was all that Jules had ever known. She was, as people liked to say, Maldon born and bred.

She went to primary school there, with the same people she went to secondary school with and the same people she would have gone on to college with had she not fallen pregnant with Austin when she was sixteen.

That was when her life took a different path from what she'd planned.

Back then, she'd thought she was in love. Now she realised how ludicrous and naïve that was.

Damien – Austin's father – was three years older and had his own car, and that had been enough for Jules to believe he was mature and adult. Someone she could trust. She had been wrong. He was a child in a man's body, and eleven years later he hadn't even met his own son. As soon as he had learned

Jules wanted to keep the baby, he packed up and left Maldon. No apologies, no letter, just a message from his friend, saying he'd had a great opportunity, and it was best if she didn't count on him coming back. The man she trusted and believed she had loved left Jules to bring up Austin on her own at her parents' house. That hadn't been easy for anyone.

Jules knew the rumours that whispered their way up and down the street when Austin was born – what a shame it was that such a clever girl had let herself go down that route. How she had ruined her life. How the baby would never have a good life, with a mother her age raising him. And when she was first pregnant, Jules had worried that perhaps they were right. She didn't know what she was doing. She couldn't even load the dishwasher without her mum telling her she'd done it wrong. How was she going to raise a child? But that first time she held Austin in her arms, Jules realised how wrong all the gossips were. This baby was going to have everything, she would make sure of it. And as far as she was concerned, she hadn't ruined her life. She had just given herself more to live for.

Unfortunately, her parents didn't agree. Not that they didn't love Austin, or Jules, but the whispering got to them. Neighbours they had known all their lives gossiped behind their backs. Women with whom her mother had held long-standing relationships simply stopped calling. The constant sly comments and subtle digs that Jules could happily let go burrowed into them, gnawing away. And so, just one week after Jules's eighteenth birthday, when Austin was a year old, they moved away from Maldon to Danbury.

In the grand scheme of things, Danbury really wasn't that far away. The village was less than ten miles down winding country roads. But it wasn't about physical distance, it was about the emotional one. They had separated themselves from her and said, without words, that they agreed with everything the gossips said. But Jules didn't let it bring her down. Instead, it lit a fire within her, the likes of which she had never known.

From that day, even more than when Austin had been born, Jules knew she needed to make something of herself. She needed to show her son what supportive parents did. So she went back to school, finished her A levels, then got onto a teacher training course, finding a placement in Maldon. Since then, she hadn't looked back. She had changed jobs twice, both times to schools in Maldon, and now worked at a private school on the outskirts of town, where the classes were small and the holidays even longer than Austin's. Her life was good. And she didn't need a man to prove what she was worth. She'd already proved that to herself a thousand times over.

The White Horse was at the top of town, just by the bus stop. The hotel had a large open area that, during Christmas time, was decorated with fairy lights which turned it into a winter wonderland, and in the summer offered people a space out in the cooler air to sip on their drinks.

When Vicky and Jules arrived at the pub, ready for a quiet evening meal, Sophie was there waiting, wearing an amazingly tiny dress. She was the youngest member of the book club, who worked with one of the other members at a local coffee shop by the river. Technically, Sophie wasn't exactly single, but given that all her relationships were a disaster waiting to happen, the club was unanimous that she fitted the bill of a lonely heart. This latest guy was constantly asking for money, and for her to pick him up from random country pubs at obscene hours. And for some reason, Sophie insisted it was okay. Yet Jules had barely even sat down when Sophie picked up from where she had left off at Book Club, launching into all the disastrous things her boyfriend had done that week.

"He's an artist. It's just what artists are like. And I don't mind most of the time. I like that he needs me."

Jules bit down on her lip.

"How about we don't talk about men at all?" she said, as Vicky mentioned all the wonderful things Oliver had done for her, and how good a boyfriend he was in comparison. "Did anyone watch that latest Ryan Gosling film? Did you like it?"

Conversation flowed between the three as Vicky ordered a bottle of wine for them to share. For a while they talked about films and television shows, then about Austin starting school and the new takeover that was happening in the hospital where Vicky worked.

With the main courses finished, the waiter was clearing away the plates when a man with a guitar tapped on a microphone. A sign the band was about to start, and Jules should head off home.

"You can't go now. We haven't even had dessert," Sophie protested.

"I really can't eat any more. I'm full."

"Then just get a drink?" Vicky countered. "If we walk out now, the band are going to think it's because we think they're terrible. We can't do that. They look nervous enough as it is."

With a twist of her neck, Jules studied the band that had now started playing. The lead singer had crouched down so low that his neck was tipped back, and he was singing up to the microphone, rather than down into it. He didn't look nervous to her. He looked like he was having a great time, but Vicky was likely right about it being rude to leave straight after they had started playing. She'd get one more drink and stretch it out for two or three songs. Hopefully that way it wouldn't look too obvious when she was leaving.

Jules was about to go to the bar when Vicky lowered her voice into a hiss.

"Okay, don't look now, but that guy at the bar is definitely checking you out." Vicky held her wine glass above her mouth as she spoke. "Seriously."

"Wow, he is definitely looking at you," Sophie seconded with a less-than-subtle look straight at the guy. "And he's hot. Too old for me, but hot."

Vicky glowered at her. "He's not old, you're just young. Besides, it's not you he's looking at. It's Jules."

"Can you both stop staring at him? He's probably just trying to enjoy a quiet night watching a band, that's all." Jules sipped her drink and resisted the urge to look at the poor man they were gossiping about. There was a good chance he was looking in their direction, but not at her unless he'd noticed something like a label sticking out the back of her top. Not with the young, gorgeous Sophie next to her, and Vicky with her flame red hair.

While Jules never considered herself unattractive, she had never seen herself as anything more than normal looking. Normal nice face. Normal nice figure. But somehow she had landed herself with an obscenely attractive group of friends. They were all so different, from their hair and skin colour to their dress sense and figures, but her friends were unequivocally stunning. As such, she was confident that whoever this mystery man was looking at, it was not her.

"Seriously, he is gorgeous," Vicky groaned.

Despite her better judgement, Jules threw a quick glance over her shoulder, only to turn immediately back to the girls.

"You cannot mean the guy at the other end?" she said. "The one on his own."

"Yes!"

Sophie shook her head and laughed. "Honestly? He was not looking at me."

Although Jules had only offered the man a fleeting glance,

she had seen more than enough to know one thing was for certain: he was well out of her league. The expensive jacket, the well-groomed hair. She saw his type here regularly enough – the boating types, who came for a quick break in the UK before hurrying off to whichever part of the Mediterranean they favoured. Most of them had a house in London and at least two other capital cities, and one on an island, too. There was no chance someone like that would be interested in a primary school teacher. A single mum, who needed a lodger to make ends meet each month. The fact her friends could think anyone like that could want anything to do with her was, quite frankly, ridiculous.

Clearing her throat, she attempted to divert the conversation.

"So, Sophie, what are your plans—"

"Is he standing up?" Sophie's voice was an urgent whisper, cutting straight over Jules. "He is. He's standing up."

An internal groan reverberated through Jules's lungs.

"He's probably going to use the bathroom."

"He's not," Vicky replied. "The bathrooms are the other direction. He's coming this way."

"Then he's probably going to get a drink or to speak to someone."

She wanted the others to say something, to confirm that she was right, and he was in fact moving elsewhere, but their eyes bulged. Vicky straightened her back, while Sophie let out a small squeak as a tall figure appeared at the end of their table.

"Hello? Can I help you?"

Vicky was the one that spoke, while Jules kept her eyes fixed on her wineglass. She didn't know why she didn't want to look up. Probably for the man's sake. After all, he was about to make a complete fool of himself, asking to buy either Vicky or Sophie a drink, when both of them had boyfriends.

A slight pause followed before he cleared his throat.

"Umm, yes." He coughed again for a second time. "I hope you don't think I'm impertinent, but I was hoping I could buy your friend here a drink."

There it was, Jules thought. He had gone for Sophie. The young, skinny blonde that fit the stereotypical standard of mainstream beauty to a tee. And it wasn't like Sophie enjoyed knocking guys back. She was far too sweet for that. She would get all embarrassed and probably ask him to sit down with them just so he didn't feel too awkward. It was a disaster waiting to unfold.

So, with her breath held, Jules waited for the inevitable rejection. Only ten seconds passed, and no one said anything.

"Jules," Vicky hissed.

That was when Jules lifted her gaze and saw he was staring straight at her. Beautiful, big brown eyes that were staring directly into hers.

"So, what do you think?" His voice had a deep tone that could easily melt a person. "May I buy you a drink?'

CHAPTER 3

It was obscenely embarrassing. Sophie and Vicky got up, giggling to each other, while saying some nonsense about wanting to be closer to the band, and all the while Jules was staring at them, with her most desperately pleading eyes. And they saw. She knew they saw. But they still didn't stay.

"Have fun!" Vicky offered one last smirk as she disappeared, leaving Jules alone with the strange man. Now that he was next to her, and she was actually looking at him, it was impossible not to notice how good-looking he was. His deep-set eyes were as dark as his jet-black hair, but rather than sitting down in one of the seats Sophie and Vicky had freed, he remained standing.

"Sorry, you didn't actually answer my question. Your friends seemed to railroad the situation, and I don't want to be presumptuous or pester you. I should go. This was a bad idea. I just thought I'd take a chance."

Jules pressed her lips tightly together. So this was his go-to chat up line? Being obscenely polite and slightly bashful. No doubt it worked. After all, it was definitely charming, if a little long-winded. Thirty seconds later and he was still going.

"I am pestering you, aren't I?" he said, shaking his head. "I… It's been a long time since I've tried to do this, you know, buy a woman a drink. I'm guessing I'm going about it all wrong."

His cheeks pinked ever so slightly, but due to the contrast with his hair, it was extremely noticeable. While Jules still suspected there was a chat up line at play, she conceded. She could always drink quickly.

"It's fine," Jules said finally. "Why don't you sit down? And in answer to your question, yes, I'd quite like another drink."

His sigh of relief was audible as he took a seat opposite Jules.

"The same again?" he said, gesturing to the empty bottle of wine in the ice cooler that the girls had polished off during their meal.

"A glass would be fine," she said.

With a wave of his hand, the man attracted a waiter.

"We'll have another bottle, we can share it," he said with a glance to Jules, before he turned his attention back to the waiter. "And while you're at it, can you take the last bottle off their bill and put it on mine?"

"You don't have to do that." Jules felt her muscles tighten. Over generosity wasn't a good sign in her books. It meant he was trying to cover something. Then again, it wasn't like she couldn't do with knocking a bit of money off the bill.

"Honestly, I don't mind. I owe your friends for giving me some space to talk to you. Although they don't seem to be enjoying the music that much."

Jules looked over her shoulder to where Sophie and Vicky were standing by the band, although they weren't dancing, or watching them, or even talking to each other.

Instead, they were both staring fixedly at Jules and the stranger.

A small chuckle escaped from her lips, which was reciprocated by the stranger seated opposite her.

"I'm sorry, I haven't even told you my name. I'm Nate."

He stretched out his hand, which Jules took and shook. Noting the lack of a wedding band on his finger.

A few years ago, Jules found herself chatting with a man in a similar situation. He had been pleasant enough and easy to talk to, given that they had similar taste in music and books. But then, when the night ended and he'd asked for her number, he had taken out his phone and she'd seen the picture of a woman and child on the lock screen, and when she'd glanced down at his hand, she'd noticed the wedding ring, firmly embedded in his finger.

"It's complicated," he'd said, as if that was an explanation.

"No, it's not," Jules had replied before turning around and leaving. Now a wedding ring was one of the first things she checked. Nate's hands were completely empty, and now that he had got past the initial terror of asking her for a drink, he had relaxed considerably.

"I'm Jules," she said as she dropped his hand.

"Well, Jules, it's very nice to meet you. You are actually the first person in Maldon, other than the bartender, I know the name of."

"Really?"

"Really."

"So you're visiting?"

"Actually, I've just moved here. Well, I'm still in the process of doing so. It's just taking a little longer than expected. So I'm staying a couple of nights at the pub while I get everything sorted at the place I'm renting. But I should be in by the end of next week."

"Moving to Maldon, wow." She didn't mean to sound derogatory in her comment. She loved the town, and had never had any great desire to leave, but if she could choose anywhere in the world to pack up and move to, she wasn't sure it would be Maldon.

Thankfully, Nate smiled at her response. "I take it you've been here awhile? Great, you can tell me all the places I need to go and the best things to avoid."

"Well, that's a long list. It's a good job you got a bottle of wine."

"I can get a crate if you think it's needed."

"Hey, it's not that bad!"

Once again, Nate chuckled and Jules couldn't help but feel her cheeks rise in response. Even if it was just a couple of drinks they were going to share, it was nice to talk to someone different now and again.

"So, what do you do for work?" Jules asked. She may have been out of the dating game forever, but that seemed like a pretty safe bet to go with. Apparently Nate disagreed.

"Do you mind if we don't talk about work? I feel like I've spent the last few days with nothing but work. Let's talk about something different. Favourite bands, television shows, vegetables."

"Vegetables?"

"I don't know. I'm grasping at straws here!"

The longer they talked, the more Jules laughed. People – by which she mainly meant Vicky – had always told Jules she had a strange sense of humour, but she and Nate seemed remarkably in tune. By the time they had finished their first glass of wine, they were already exchanging favourite cat memes, and firing off quotes from their favourite Ryan Reynolds films. Once, she even found herself wiping back the tears as she struggled to breathe. Nate, she discovered, was terrible at doing impressions.

It was after that bout of laughter, when they had finally regained their composure, that Nate's smile dropped into a far more serious expression.

"I'm so glad I asked you for a drink. You know, it took me forever. I'd been plucking up courage since I saw you and your friends walk in."

Jules stopped, the tears of laughter having come to an abrupt halt. She looked Nate straight in the eyes. They were unusually coloured eyes, she decided. Not as dark as she'd first thought. Mostly brown, but with flecks of green. Hazel, perhaps? And what did it say of her that she had barely even clocked him when she came in? The fact that anyone could overlook a man like Nate seemed an impossibility.

"Why did you ask me for a drink?" she said, voicing the words she had been thinking since he sat down. "Why not Vicky, or Sophie?"

"Your friends?" he said.

"Yes."

"Because I didn't want to."

Jules raised her eyebrows. That wasn't an acceptable answer, and if he'd learned nothing else about her from the last hour of chatting, he should have realised that would not cut it.

"Really, why?" She pressed.

Rather than replying, Nate topped up both of their glasses and rested his hands on the table.

"You were the one perfectly at ease in your own skin."

"Is that right?"

"It is. Your friend, the redhead – which one is that?"

"Vicky."

"Right. Vicky is all about the attention. The way her eyes

constantly move, all the flicking of the hair, the head back when she laughs. Don't get me wrong, I'm sure she's lovely, but I've been with the drama queen type before, and we don't blend well."

It wasn't the first time someone had called Vicky a drama queen, but it also wasn't a piece of information Jules was going to pass on.

"And Sophie?"

"The other one? Who's young enough to be my daughter?"

"She's not that young. She's only five years younger than me."

"Well, you had something more mature about you then. More put together. Like someone who has their life in order. You walked in, not bothered about seeing who else was here, or making small talk with anyone else. You'd come to be with your friends. That was it."

"And so you thought you'd disturb that evening?" She pursed her lips, waiting for that slight pink of a blush to colour Nate's cheeks, and she was not disappointed.

"When you put it like that, it makes me sound like an arse. But there was something about your ease that made me think you were the type of person I wanted to get to know." He leaned back in his seat and took a long sip from his glass. "Does that answer your question?"

Following suit, Jules took a mouthful of her drink while pondering his question. She was grateful he hadn't come out with a line about her being the most beautiful of the three, when it blatantly wasn't true, and he had certainly hit the nail on the head with his character assessments of Vicky. But did Jules really have her act together? It didn't feel like it a lot of the time, juggling all of Austin's activities with her own commitments. The stack of waiting bills, and the itemised shopping list to ensure they didn't go over budget, didn't feel like someone who had their life all sorted. But then she was organised, and stayed on top of things, and had never missed a deadline yet.

"I guess it does," she replied.

For a second, neither of them spoke. It was the first silence to infiltrate their conversation all night. Although it wasn't an awkward silence. There was something amazingly calming about it. Like his presence somehow made it easier to think. Her hands were resting on the table, and without a word, Nate lifted his own, placed them on top of hers, and interlocked their fingers.

At any other time in her life, Jules would have thought it ridiculous. The act of holding hands with a man she had only just met in the middle of a crowded pub was not something she would ever do. Or think anyone else should do either. But nothing felt ridiculous about her situation. It felt easy. Perfect. Fated almost.

"I can't believe I almost didn't come down for a drink tonight," Nate said, breaking the silence. As he did, Jules glanced down at the large watch on his wrist, only to jerk back in surprise.

"How is it that time already?" Her pulse soared as she checked her watch just to make sure. "I was meant to be back by ten-thirty." She was on her feet.

"I'm so sorry. I didn't mean to keep you."

"No, it's fine. It's fine. Where are the girls?"

Somewhere during their conversation, Jules had stopped thinking about Vicky and Sophie and been focused entirely on Nate. However, now she had no idea where they were.

Nate was also on his feet. "I'll walk you outside. I can stay with you until you find them. Make sure they're okay."

It didn't take long to find her friends at all. They were huddled together near the archway outside.

"Jules!" They were less than subtle as they looked at the pair and giggled. "You two looked like you were having fun."

The fear Jules had felt that her friends had somehow disappeared was immediately replaced with the desire to offer them some very choice words. Instead, she turned her back to them and looked at Nate.

"So..." Nate let the rest of his sentence drift into nothing.

"So..." Jules responded.

The night was warm enough, but a cool breeze was causing the skin on her arms to prickle. She rubbed her hands together.

"You're cold. Here, take my jacket." He shifted his arm to remove it, but Jules stopped him.

"It's fine, honestly. I don't have a long walk."

"Then maybe I'll walk back with you?"

A group of youngsters tumbled out of the pub beside them, and Nate slipped his arm around Jules's waist and pulled her over to the side.

The pressure of his grip caused an unexpected dizziness. A light-headedness that could have come from the wine, only she hadn't been feeling it until the exact moment of his touch. And then, with his hands around her waist, Jules felt an obscene level of stability. The dizziness was still there, but it wasn't just her head that was spinning. It was her heart. As ridiculous as it sounded, they fit together perfectly.

They were closer than they had been all night. So close that Jules could feel the warmth radiating from him. Could she really let him walk her home? Then what? He'd probably expect her to invite him in, and there was no chance that was going to happen. The reality of what she was setting herself up for kicked the dizziness hurriedly away.

"I don't think that's a good idea."

"Please don't tell me you have an angry husband who's about to come after me?"

"No, no husband."

"Boyfriend?"

"I am utterly single."

The smile twitched on his lips. "I should have probably checked that before."

"It would have been a good place to start." Her heart thudded behind her ribs. Her throat drying as she spoke. "And you?"

A pause formed at the end of her question, and for a fretful moment, she feared that he was about to tell her he was in a relationship. This perfect, natural ease that made her feel like she had known him for years, not for a couple of hours.

"I am single. And if we're both single, I can take you for dinner? If you would like."

It was her turn to pause. "Dinners are complicated for me. I don't usually come out like this. I have a child. A son."

Nate nodded. This was it, Jules thought. This was the moment where he kissed her on the lips, told her it had been a lovely evening, but she was probably right. Anything more than that would get complicated. Instead, he pursed his lips together.

"Isn't that a coincidence? I'm great with kids. Though I don't want to take him for dinner yet. Let's give it a couple of weeks first, shall we?"

A lump had formed in Jules's throat. One, she had no idea how she was going to get rid of until Nate tightened his grip around her waist.

"In a minute, you're going to give me your phone and I'm going to put my number in. But before that, if it's alright with you, I'm going to kiss you?'

CHAPTER 4

Jules had been awake for hours. Tossing and turning and unable to settle. It was the same at the start of every academic year. Why, after four years of doing the same job, she still had massive nerves on the first day back after the summer, she couldn't explain, but once again, they were there. And this year they were even worse because there was Austin to worry about too. Annoyingly he was starting back today as well, meaning she couldn't walk with him on his first day at secondary school.

"Are you sure you know which gate you're going in through?" Jules asked him as she dropped a piece of bread into the toaster. "I'm sure one of the other parents won't mind walking in with you this once to make sure you've got your bearings."

"Mum, listen," Austin put his spoon down on the table next to his bowl of cereal. When he was a baby, Jules hated how much he looked like his father. He'd been born with the same round face and chubby cheeks. And the exact shade of blue eyes that his father had possessed. But after a few days, his eyes had darkened to brown and his face had grown longer and less round, and now as he was starting secondary school, Jules could see more of herself in her son than ever before. "I know you're stressed, but honestly, I don't need anyone to walk me in. Me and all the boys are going together. We're meeting at the top of the high street. Besides, I've been to the school before, remember? We had taster days and the Year 5 science day. I pretty much know my way around it already."

For most eleven-year-olds, saying that they knew their way around a secondary school after only two visits would have sounded like a ludicrous exaggeration, or at least a distinct overconfidence in their ability. But Austin wasn't like that. He had a phenomenal memory. Numbers, dates, buildings, names. Two visits probably were enough for him to get a good bearing on the place. So if Austin said he knew his way around the school, Jules didn't doubt him for one second.

"Okay. Alright. And when are you meeting the others?"

"Eight-fifteen. So I'll leave the house at the same time as you. As it's only a ten-minute walk, it's going to give us plenty of time, so you can really stop stressing."

When he was young, Jules had assumed all the comments about Austin being extremely bright were the normal compliments paid to new parents. Sure, he had no problem stacking bricks on top of each other or finding the right holes to push the different shapes through, but they were children's toys and he was just doing what they were designed for. Then, when he could speak, and identify various sea creatures from the different layers of the oceans, she had once again thought this was something all children with a keen interest in marine life did. It wasn't until he started primary school and was reading books two years above his expected age that she realised people weren't making their comments out of politeness. Austin was a bright child. Unusually bright.

"Don't forget that if you want to sign up for the chess club, they said it's only got limited spaces," Jules said, grabbing the butter as the toast popped out of the toaster. Unexpectedly, Austin huffed. "What, you love chess, don't you?"

"Yeah. But I don't think I'm going to join the school team."

"Why not?"

"Because the team captain is Eddie Carter. You know, he went to the same primary school and was three years above me. I beat him twice when he was in Year 6, so if he's the best they've got, I don't think there's gonna be much competition. Besides, I think I want to join the debate team."

"Debate team?" Jules sat down at the table opposite and took a bite of her toast. Debate definitely sounded more fun than chess club, but she didn't envy anyone who went up against her son. "How come you want to do that now?"

Austin waited until he had finished his mouthful of cereal before he spoke.

"To start with, you get a day off timetable once a term for the meets, and then there's a trip to the States at the end of the year, provided we get through the heats, which they've done for the last four years, so we're bound to. It's at one of the big universities, and you go up against all these teams from different countries around the world. That's the kind of competition I want. Actual competition."

"A competition in America? Wow." Jules tried to keep her voice as neutral as possible, despite the lump that was forming in her throat. Still, she didn't need to speak. Austin knew exactly what she was thinking.

"You don't need to worry about the money, Mum. It's not until June. And I was thinking I could get a job. I know they give paper rounds out to people in Year 7. That gives me ten months to help save up."

Jules smiled, but she could feel it straining her cheeks. She didn't know how much a paper round paid, but she very much doubted it would be enough to save for a school trip to the USA. Not to mention the fact the school would start asking for deposits soon. Extra money she didn't have.

"Well, I'm sure that sounds great, but don't discount all the other clubs yet. You never know, they might have some really great chess players joining this year."

"I'm not discounting them. I've decided I'm going to join a sports team too."

At this, Jules nearly choked on her toast. Austin had received exemplary reports in every subject throughout primary school, with the one exception: P.E. Although they were always positive, comments like *tries hard and enthusiastic* were common in these reports, and as a teacher, Jules was well aware of the underlying meaning. Yes, he tried hard, but he couldn't catch a ball half the time. The fact that he would think he would find a place on a secondary school team left her more than a little confused.

"Don't worry." He read her expression with humour. "I know I'm rubbish. But if I want a top university to take me seriously, I need to show that I'm a rounded student. That means sports. I'm not planning on playing. Just joining and being a substitute now and again."

Jules wasn't sure how to respond and whether she should be concerned by the fact her son was already thinking about universities, or that he thought that was all being on a sports team would involve. Though for now, she chose to ignore it all.

"Well, sounds like you've got everything planned. Now hurry up with that breakfast. You still need to get dressed."

With one more hasty scoop of his cereal, Austin stood up and crossed the room and placed his bowl in the dishwasher.

No sooner was Austin out of the kitchen than Vicky walked through the door. She had spent Sunday on a double shift, which included the night one too, and Jules hadn't expected her to be up this early, but she should have known she'd never let Austin leave for his first day of secondary school without saying goodbye.

"You look rough," she said, as she stole a half a slice of toast from Jules's plate. "Pre-school jitters?"

"Yup."

"It'll be fine. Just seen Austin. He looks cool as a cucumber."

"When isn't he?"

"True."

Vicky was still chewing on her toast when she spoke again.

"So, Nate, have you heard from him?"

It was both a blessing and annoyance that Vicky had been working on Sunday. Had she been home, she would probably have badgered Jules for more information about Nate the same way she'd done on the walk back from the pub. But unusually for Jules, she wanted to talk about it.

"Maybe?" she replied coyly.

"Maybe. What does that mean?"

Jules's heart fluttered as she jumped to her feet, checked that Austin wasn't anywhere in earshot, then closed the door just in case.

"He rang me last night."

"Rang you? Straight to telephone calls. No texts?"

"There've been texts too. On Friday night after we got back from the pub. And Saturday. Sunday morning too. But it was late last night, and he was in his hotel room, and he said he just wanted to hear my voice. I mean, it's cheesy, obviously. I'm not reading too much into it."

"Are you serious? You don't want to read much into it, but you're talking on the phone. What did he talk about? Or was it less talking and more... If you get my drift?"

Jules thumped her friend on the arm. "No, there was none of that. It was just chatting. He asked me what type of food I liked, for when he takes me out for dinner."

"Which is going to be when, exactly?"

Jules drew in a lungful of air. She had considered not mentioning it to Vicky, because she knew she'd get overly excited and it would only make matters worse when the whole thing fizzled into nothing. But she could do with Vicky babysitting, assuming she wasn't working or out with Oliver.

"Friday."

It didn't matter how much she tried to suppress her grin, she couldn't. And it didn't help that Vicky jumped up and down on the spot and squealed. That was the exact moment when Austin appeared in the room.

"What are you doing?" He looked at them equally accusingly.

"Your mum's got a date," Vicky said.

Austin's eyes bugged. "Seriously? With who?"

Jules shot a glare at her friend. She and Austin didn't have secrets, but mainly because there was nothing to be secretive about. She had made sure she was open with him, even on silly things like celebrity crushes, or bad days she'd had a work, because she knew that if she wasn't open with her son, then he'd never be open with her. As it was, he told her everything, or at least it felt that way. She knew when he'd made a new friend or fallen out with an old one. Not that it happened often. She knew which teachers were still giving him work that was far too easy and who in the class had been bullying other people. But they had never had a conversation like this. Nerves churned through her. Would he respond badly, feeling like he was being usurped as the only man in her life? Would this thing with Nate be over before it had started?

But rather than any of that, he sat back down in his chair.

"So come on. Tell us about him. It is a him, right? I don't mind if it's not."

"Yes, it's a him. His name is Nate." Jules was proud of her son for his openness.

"Nate. Short for Nathan or Nathaniel?"

"I don't know?" Jules felt the churn of dread returning.

"You don't know what his name is?"

"I know his name. His name is Nate. I just don't know what it's short for."

"Okay, what about surname? If I know his surname, then I can probably search and find his actual first name."

"I am not giving you his surname so that you can stalk my potential date," Jules said, confused at how quickly this conversation had derailed.

"You don't know it, do you?" Austin continued. "You're going on a date with a man whose name you don't really know at all."

"Can we just move the conversation away from his name? In fact, can we move the conversation away from my dating life altogether?"

"We will. I've just a few more questions," Austin reminded her more of a lawyer during a court interrogation than her son. Jules cast a glance and Vicky, who was still standing in the corner, a wide smirk on her face. There was no chance she was going to come to her rescue.

"Fine, one more question," Jules said.

"What does he do?" Austin asked.

"Business, actually. He's just opened a branch in Maldon. Hence he's moved."

"Okay, that sounds good. What kind of business is it?"

Jules was once again stumped. She tried to bring it up, but only briefly. Nate hadn't wanted to talk about work on the phone to her last night, and she hadn't been keen to talk about her job either, given how she was about to go back after the long break, so it seemed fine. Until now. Now it felt strange. Her silence filled the kitchen.

"So, is there anything you actually learned about him?" Austin asked, his level of cynicism far greater than fitting for an eleven-year-old.

"Yes, I learned that he has a daughter, actually."

At this, Vicky's jaw dropped.

"You didn't say when we walked home. Did you know that then? When did you find that out?"

It was Jules's turn to look at her friend with scepticism.

"On the phone last night. He said he'd been chatting to his daughter before he rang me. I don't know why you're both looking at me like that. People our age have children. I have a child. What is that so surprising?"

"It's just surprising that you're calm about it," Vicky said. "You spoke to him for nearly two hours on Saturday night, and you didn't find out that he had a child? Don't you think that's something you should mention to a woman you give your phone number to?"

"I don't know. I didn't bring up Austin until the very end of the evening?"

"You didn't? I'm offended," Austin mocked, though Jules didn't have a chance to reply before Vicky continued.

"How old is she? Does she live with him?"

"I don't know. I didn't want to press. But I mentioned

Austin was starting secondary school, and he said that she'll be there in a couple of years. So I guess she's about nine."

Once again, Vicky was ready with another question, but Jules cut her off before she could speak.

"Can we stop this? There is nothing to talk about right now and I will keep you informed when and only if appropriate. Now, can we please all get out of the kitchen? We've got places to be.'

CHAPTER 5

Jules's first job had been at the local primary school, and she'd loved it. Her class was lively – that was the word she used most frequently at parents' evening to describe it back then. Lively, enthusiastic, energetic. Words that most discerning parents could figure out meant their little ones would not keep quiet or sit and listen, but that didn't mean she hadn't loved it. Her second job had been very similar. Cheeky classes that would happily offer her red herrings to avoid doing any maths or English all day. But when a job opened at St Catherine's preparatory school, Jules decided, on a whim, to apply.

Before the interview, she'd never considered working at a prep school and the first thing that struck her when she walked through the cast-iron gates were the uniforms. Boater hats, duffel coats, shirts with wide collars which sat perfectly beneath the pinafore dresses the girls wore. Knee-length white socks. Sparkling shoes. Yes, those were what she noticed first.

The second thing was the class sizes. When she took up the position, she went – what felt like overnight – from teaching a class of thirty-two to a class of twelve.

Not that the job was perfect. There were days when she desperately missed her old colleagues, and the banter that all the different characters in her old class offered her. Not to mention the after-school activities meant she was home a lot later than she would have liked. But now she had settled in with her Year 2 class of six- and seven-year-olds, and she couldn't imagine working anywhere else.

"Jules, over here?"

Jules spotted the hand waving across the staff room. Jules made her way between the chairs and past the coffee tables and took a seat next to Frances. The Year 6 teacher was both the longest and oldest employee at St Catherine's. Having been in the job longer than Jules had been alive, there wasn't anything Frances hadn't seen in teaching. The former head of the school was an outward cynic, but inward softie. Every year she insisted it was going to be her last, and yet there she was, sixty-five and still donning fancy-dress each Christmas for the teachers' pantomime. Despite the differences between the pair, Frances was, without a doubt, Jules's best work buddy.

"At least this is the last time I'm going to have to do one of these start-of-year inset sessions," Frances groaned as Jules sat down.

"You know you said that last year. And the year before."

"Well, this time I mean it. I'm going to buy a villa in Italy. You know you can buy them for a pound in some places?"

"Is that right?" Every year Frances had a different retirement plan, and every year she "accidentally" missed the resignation date, and come September was back again. "So, did you have a good holiday? Do anything exciting?" Jules asked, keen to catch up after all the weeks away.

"I cleared out the attic," Frances said. "That was pretty exciting. Found half a mummified mouse up there."

"*Half* a mouse?"

"Your guess is as good as mine. And I went to the caravan in Tenby, which was nice. It rained five out of the six days, so I stayed inside and read, which is exactly what I would have done if I'd stayed home, but it was Welsh rain, so that was different. Which reminds me, have you seen the new assistant head?"

Jules wasn't sure why talking about her rainy holiday in Tenby reminded Frances of the new assistant head but given how her mind was occupied with so many other things for the day, it didn't seem worth asking. Still, Frances wasn't quite done. "I'd get in there quick, if I were you. Sonia on reception is already taking bets as to which of you young, single ones he's going to take out for a drink first. She has a friend of a friend who worked at his last school, and apparently he finished his last relationship six months ago. Sounds like good timing."

While Frances was nowhere near as bad as Vicky at nagging Jules about the relationship market, she sensed that this could develop into something more if she didn't nip it in the bud now.

"Don't go there. You know I'm not interested. Besides, I might not be completely single anymore."

"You say that, but you haven't seen him yet. I'm not saying he's enough to turn me, but not far off." Jules laughed at the comment, grateful that Frances hadn't asked her any more about her fledgling relationship. After failing the morning interrogation with Vicky and Austin so spectacularly, she wasn't sure she could cope with another set of questions like that.

"Ah, here come the bosses."

All eyes turned to the double doors as senior management began to filter through. The head of the curriculum came first, followed by the school head, Mrs Dawn Dowling. And then he followed.

"See, I told you."

He was attractive. Dark hair. Bright blue eyes. But even if she hadn't met Nate, Jules would never consider starting a relationship with someone at work. Definitely not someone higher up than her. That was a recipe for disaster.

"Definitely single, too," Frances continued quietly. "I don't think he's going to stay that way for long, though."

"Well, we'll see," Jules said.

At the front of the room, the head cleared her throat and began to reel off her list of notices for the day. Given that it was the first day of the academic year, there were a lot.

"I know you all have plenty of things you want to be getting on with today, like setting up your classrooms, but please remember to respond to all emails as promptly as you can. And those of you who have new students starting in your class, the parents are coming in for a one-to-one meeting this afternoon. I have placed a schedule on the shared drive. Please check that straight away to make sure you're not caught by surprise. There's not a large intake this term, but we want to give the best impression we can for them."

After that, the notices went on. "Please ensure that you are familiar with the new computer system. There will be a training session next week. Also, there will be a staff meeting on Friday morning to discuss the upcoming school trip. This is not optional. Mid- and short-term lesson plans should be submitted to Frances by the end of the week. And finally..."

Dawn paused to flash a smile. "I'd like to introduce Mr Gethin Jones, our new assistant head."

At this the attractive Gethin stepped forwards.

"Thank you. I'm very pleased to be here." The deep Welsh accent made it clear why Frances had linked Tenby with their new manager, and a collective dreamy sigh rattled out from various people in the staff room, regardless of age. "I know you're probably expecting me to stand up here and tell you all the ideas and systems I want to introduce this year, but you've got some great things going on here and I don't plan on interfering with that at all. I'm not going to look at making any changes until I've been here a while. For now, I'm merely looking forward to getting to know you and all the fantastic students we have. So have a great start to the year everybody."

A slight pause followed, during which people looked at each other, before someone finally plucked up the courage to stand.

"I suppose that means we better get on with it." Frances pushed herself to her feet. "See you back here at lunchtime? I picked up some vegan chocolate brownies from that refill shop down the alley. Damn good."

"I'll see you back here at lunchtime," Jules said.

"I'll hold you to that. You can't spend all day in your classroom. You'll need a break."

"I will," Jules said, genuinely hoping to try.

This was Jules's second year in the same classroom, and after a year of trying out new seating arrangements and table setups, she finally had it how she liked it. But that didn't mean there weren't jobs to do today. All the backing paper needed replacing on the boards, and she needed to print out her student names, cut them out, laminate them, and stick them to the board ready to move up and down the rainbow according to how well they were behaving during lesson time. So far, she had only ever had two students reach a thundercloud. Most sat on the sunshine level or rainbow level, occasionally moving to a shooting star. Even a slight threat of moving them down onto a cloud was normally enough for them to rapidly improve their behaviour.

As instructed, Jules checked the schedule to see when she would be meeting her new parents and students. She normally had one or two new starters, but this year there were three. Two boys and one girl. Thankfully, all the meetings were scheduled after lunch, meaning she had the morning to get on with her work.

Despite Frances's warning, time disappeared, and Jules decided against heading to the staffroom for lunch. She would have felt bad, particularly about the brownie, although she was almost certain Frances would be working in her room too. Still, she wasn't prepared for the rap on the door that told Jules it was already time for her first meeting.

"Come in, come in." Jules offered her widest smile as she opened the door to her first new student and his parents. "Please take a seat."

The seats she pointed at were the same pint-sized pieces of furniture that the children sat on in lessons. While Jules had a proper adult-size chair, there was only one, and so she always conducted meetings around one of the children's tables. Besides, she was used to it now. She spent half her life with her knees tucked under her chin when she sat in front of the class and taught them phonics or basic fractions. But it was always amusing, seeing how parents coped with these tiny chairs.

The first boy, Ethan, had moved from another school in Maldon, and his dads were very keen on knowing the ins and outs of the academic rigour of the school. The second student arrived with his parents, just five minutes after Ethan and his dads had left and were far more concerned about the holistic side of things.

"We see you have a choice of vegetarian options on the lunch menu," the mother said, glancing at her notebook as she ticked off her comments one by one. "But we saw nothing about vegan meals. I assume that this will be accommodated?"

Jules smiled. "I will definitely make a note to look into that," she said. "Do you have any other questions?"

"Yes, I wondered what the school's mindfulness practices were and how much time is set aside each day for meditation."

The second meeting left Jules even more exhausted, but it was frustrating that the third ones weren't there waiting, even though she had overrun. She checked her watch. They were late. After a brief contemplation, she decided she'd wait in her classroom for five minutes. If they weren't there then, she'd go down to the school office and see if they had had a phone call. It was possible they had decided to pull the children out at the last minute. It had happened before.

Giving herself a few more minutes to fix up her display boards, she was standing on one of the small stools, fixing the border to her backing paper, when there was a knock on the door.

"Sorry we're late. We had a nightmare parking."

Jules stepped down off the stool and turned to the door, where a woman in her early thirties was dressed in a light cream suit and wearing the type of heels that made her dizzy just looking at them.

"It's fine. It's fine to come in," Jules said. "You must be Evie's mum."

The woman walked towards Jules's desk, while behind her trailed a young girl, dressed immaculately, as she held onto her father's hand.

Given that Jules's attention was solely fixed on the girl – to whom she offered her widest smile – she didn't immediately notice the hand that Evie was holding onto, and it was only as her eyes moved upwards from the little girl that they landed on her father. Tall, with brown eyes flecked with green. Jules's heart leapt in her chest.

"Nate?'

CHAPTER 6

Jules was rooted to the spot. Her heart pounding in her chest, her breath so ragged, it was a near miracle she hadn't passed out already. There was no mistaking it now. It was definitely Nate, with his gorgeous eyes and perfect hair, although he looked substantially paler than when she had first met him.

"I'm sorry, you already know my husband?" Evie's mum was walking forwards, shaking Jules's hand. "You must be one of the teachers who showed him around in the holiday? I'm sorry we couldn't come to the open day, but the move was slightly last minute, wasn't it, darling?"

Jules's cheeks were burning, the heat prickling behind her eyes. She could hear the woman talking, but it was peripheral. Her gaze was still locked on Nate. What was that word she had used? Her husband. Nate, Nathaniel, Nathan, whoever he was. He was married. She had kissed a married man.

"Sorry," she said, turning back to the wife.

"Sorry?"

"Yes, sorry, yes. That was it. The open day. I showed

him round then." Her cheeks were aching as she forced herself to smile, but the muscles were resisting her with everything they had. With a deep breath in, she reminded herself that she was at work. This was a meeting. A new parent, and nothing else. "I'm so glad you decided to send Evie to us."

"We're separated." Nate blurted out his first words since he had stepped foot in the room.

"Sorry?"

"Flick," he said, "She's my wife. But we're separated."

Nate's eyes were wide, pleading almost as Evie's mum – Flick, Jules had now discovered – threw him a scowl.

"I hardly think this is the time to get into semantics," she hissed.

Nate nodded rapidly. His Adam's apple bobbing up and down as he swallowed.

"I just thought it might be important, you know, for documentation and letters and things. The school will need to send us things separately. Because we're separated."

Flick's smile was even tighter than Jules's, and Jules noted the way the corner of her eyes were twitching as if she might erupt. However embarrassed Jules was feeling, it was a slight relief that she wasn't the only one.

"I hardly think our temporary accommodation situation is the most important thing to talk about right now, darling," Flick muttered through close teeth.

"No, no, of course not." Jules finally found her voice and channelled the teacher within her. She had a new child starting in her class, and it was her responsibility to make sure she was as happy as possible. And if the situation between the parents was as Nate had described, then the last thing she needed was her teacher coming across as scatty or uninterested. "Please, come in. Sit down. Now, Evie, I want to hear all about you. Tell me, which subjects are you most excited about?"

As the young girl was talking, Jules found it impossible not to notice how much like her father she looked. The same smile. The same deep-set eyes. She was a gorgeous young girl, but then, why wouldn't she be? Her mum was stunning. She looked like the type of woman you'd find in a magazine. Not a fashion magazine, but one of those business empire women, with a briefcase by her side, and an article about all the amazing things she'd done in her life. There was no chance this Flick was someone who'd lived in the same town all her life. No, she'd probably travelled the world.

"I like drawing," Evie said in response to Jules's question. Her smile was timid, but firmly held in place, as if this were what she knew her parents wanted her to say. "And writing stories. I've written my own stories before."

"That's fantastic. I like writing stories too. Do you think perhaps you might bring some in for me to read?" Jules leaned in as she spoke to the girl. "We actually publish a book at the end of the year with the children's stories in. Poems, too. Perhaps you could write one to go in it?"

"Can I do that?" Evie directed her question to her parents rather than to Jules. "Can I bring all my stories in?"

"If your teacher says that's okay," Flick replied. "Sorry, I've forgotten your name. I know it's written down here somewhere."

As Flick shuffled the various pieces of paper she had been given as part of the welcome pack, Jules's gaze involuntarily rose to meet Nate's. For a split second, he looked as if he was about to say something, only for Jules to beat him to it.

"It's Miss Chard. Jules Chard."

"Miss? You're not married then?" Flick's eyebrow's arched

slightly. "I hope you don't mind me asking, but you look quite young. How many years experience do you have in the job?"

"You can't ask her that." Nate's voice was sharp and on edge, an absolute contrast to the man Jules had been speaking to on Friday night, not to mention on the phone less than twenty-four hours ago. She wouldn't have even recognised it.

However, Flick didn't so much as bat an eyelid.

"I don't think there's any harm in asking. After all, we're paying a lot of money for the school fees here. I want to know that we're getting a teacher who's at the top of their game."

"I can assure you I am." Jules was having a harder and harder time keeping her smile intact. "In fact, I was nominated as one of the county's top primary school teachers at the school awards two years ago. Not that that really makes any difference. All our teachers here are extremely competent. And I like to think that we all keep each other at the top of our game, regardless of how long we have been teaching."

"See?" Flick said with a look of smug satisfaction. "There was no harm in asking."

Jules's eyes flicked to Nate. It was out of habit. After all, she would always look at both parents when she was conducting a meeting like this. Only Nate wasn't looking at her. He was looking straight down at his feet. The fact he couldn't even bear to lift his gaze caused a deep throb in her chest.

"Okay, so I'll just go through a few of the general day-to-day housekeeping things for you." Jules continued, trying to keep the conversation on track and ignore the ache of humiliation. "Then if you have any other questions, we can go through them after that, if that's alright?"

"Perfect. We're all ears." Flick said, her perfectly painted lips twisting up into a smile, which caused Jules's stomach to corkscrew with nerves. Swallowing it down, she took a deep breath in and started her normal spiel about uniform, snack requirements and the timetable.

The number of stutters and stumbles which came from Jules's mouth were even more than the first parent interview she had done as a new teacher. She stopped and hesitated constantly, and every time Flick asked a question, she would feel the flood of fear, as if she didn't know what she was talking about at all.

As for Nate, he didn't say a word.

"So, I think that's covered everything," Jules said, still panicking that she'd forgotten something vital. "Do you have any questions?"

"Not at the moment, but have I got your direct email just in case any more questions arise?" Flick asked.

"Correspondence should go through the office," Jules said, as diplomatically as she could. "If you have anything urgent and you ring through, that will be the quickest way to reach me."

"Of course, of course. Right, I think that's everything, isn't it? Unless you want to contribute, Nathaniel?"

Nathaniel. Jules looked at his hair and polished shoes. Of course, it was Nathaniel. At least she'd been able to tell Vicky and Austin if they asked, not that she had any intention of ever mentioning Nate again, let alone telling them how she'd found out his name.

"No, there's nothing I need to say right now. Like you said, I can get in touch. I'm sure I'll probably think of some things I need to clarify with you later."

Against her better judgement, Jules looked straight at Nate. Was that pleading in his eyes? It certainly looked like it. Rightly so. He was probably terrified that she was going to out at him for being a philanderer in front of his wife. No matter how much she currently despised herself for thinking she could've found a decent guy, she hated him more.

"Great, then." Jules's smile was back. "Nate, be a darling and take Evie into the car. There's just one more thing I wanted to ask Miss... What was it?"

"Chard," Jules said.

"Sorry, yes, I'm terrible with names. We'll just be a minute."

Nate stood up and took Evie's hand, but he didn't move.

"It's fine. We can wait."

"I'd rather you didn't."

There was that tone again, and even Nate flinched before turning back to Jules again.

"Well, thank you again, Miss Chard," he said, locking his eyes with hers. "We will absolutely be in contact."

Jules's heart was drumming, but she kept her tone perfectly even as she returned his gaze. "Like I said, communication is best done with reception," she said.

CHAPTER 7

With Nate and Evie heading back to the car, both women stood facing the door, listening to the sound of footsteps retreating. Even now, Jules was having trouble making sense of what had just happened. Let alone what was about to happen.

Nate was married. The man she had kissed, the man she had spoken to for hours on her phone, was married. And his child was in her class. What the hell?

Once it was clear that Nate and Evie were gone, Flick turned back to Jules.

"I'm sorry about that," she said, her smile faltering by just a fraction. "I wanted to give it a minute. I don't want Evie to overhear what I need to say."

"That's fine," Jules said, a twisting in her gut making her queasy. Did Flick know? Was that why she wanted her daughter away, so Evie didn't hear her mother laying into the woman who had kissed her dad less than seventy-two hours beforehand? A burning heat was rising to her cheeks as she tried to keep her expression neutral. "Do you want to sit down?" She pointed back to the tiny seats, aware of the strangled sound in her throat.

"Yes, I will. Thank you."

It was infuriating how perfect Flick looked even on a miniature plastic chair. It didn't look amusing or comical, the way it normally did when parents sat down. Instead, it looked edgy, like she was posing for some funky ad campaign for an extortionately priced clothes brand. Absentmindedly, Jules's gaze floated down to Flick's hands, where she noted the rings on her left ring finger. Given the size of the central diamond, it was hard to miss. She was used to seeing parents at her school wearing jewellery like that, and normally, Jules didn't take much notice. But today, that sparkly diamond, and the thin silver band of a wedding ring beneath it, made her feel physically nauseous.

"So, what is it you wanted to talk about?" Jules asked, trying to have some control over the conversation, if only initially. "If you're worried about Evie settling in, please don't be. I know lots of these children have come up together from reception, but they're a very welcoming group, and the class sizes are small. Besides, I can already see what a lovely girl she is. I'm certain she'll have absolutely no problem fitting in."

"Oh, it's not about Evie," Flick started. "Well, it is. Of course it is. As you may have gathered from my husband's initial entrance, Nate and I are going through a few difficulties."

"Oh, I'm sorry," Jules said. She wasn't sure how else to reply. Given the circumstances, that seemed like the most natural response. Though Flick waved away her concern.

"Honestly, it's not as bad as all that. He's being dramatic. All marriages go through ups and downs. I'm sure a pretty young girl such as yourself has been in enough relationships to know that."

Jules wasn't sure what aggravated her so much. Was it the fact that Flick had referred to Jules as a "pretty young girl," despite being a highly qualified, experienced educator? Or was it that Flick simply assumed that she must have had a lot of relationships? Not wanting to answer directly, Jules offered a tight-lipped smile in response.

"This is just one of those rough patches, that's all," Flick continued. "In a couple of weeks, everything will be back to normal. But at the moment, as you can imagine, my primary concern is Evie."

"Of course, of course I can." Guilt fluttered within Jules. Whatever she had been thinking about before, at the end of the day, Flick was clearly just a mother who wanted the best for her child.

"Obviously, there is so much going on for her at the minute, what with the move away from her friends and a new school. I was just really hoping you could keep an extra eye on her."

"Of course, of course I will."

"You know, if she gets upset or mentions home at all, could you just let me know?"

"Yes, absolutely."

After a deep inhale, Flick let out a long sigh. "To be honest, I'm half hoping there will be. Perhaps if Nathaniel could see the impact of his actions on our family, he might rethink what he's doing." She sniffed again before dabbing beneath her eyes. "I'm sorry. I shouldn't be burdening you with this."

Jules's guilt was on overdrive. She was a truly terrible person. At least, she felt that way.

"It's really not a burden," she insisted. "Of course, I will keep an extra eye on Evie."

"Thank you. Thank you." Flick stood up with her unfathomable grace and stretched out her hand. "Thank you again,

Miss Chard. See, I told you it just takes me a bit of time with names. I know Evie will be very lucky to have you."

With that, she turned and walked to the door.

This time it was Jules who waited until the patter of footsteps disappeared down the corridor, at which point, she turned around, marched across to her desk and slumped down in her chair.

How was this possible? She wanted to scream. How, after eleven years of not thinking a single man she had met was datable, had the first one she'd found been married? And a parent at the school she taught at? If she hadn't thought the fates were against her with love, she was certainly sure of it now.

She dropped her head onto the table then lifted it up, only to swing it down again in frustration.

"Argh!" she screamed, as she pretended to hit her head against the table. "Why? Why? Why?"

"Is everything alright there?"

The Welsh accent which came from the door had just a hint of humour amid the concern. With her hair now splayed across her face, Jules turned to see the beautiful Gethin Jones standing in the doorway. Judging from his smirk, he had been standing there for quite a while.

"I might be new to the school, but I'm not sure if the budget will stretch to new desks if this is how you're going to treat them on the first day back."

Jules straightened up and tucked her hair behind her ears the best she could.

"I'm sorry," she said, "I've just had a lot of juggling to do today, that's all."

"Anything I can help with?" Gethin walked into the room. Rather than sitting on one of the chairs, he sat on the corner of her desk. "It is my job, after all. And I'm sure it will help me get the others on side if I help sort an issue for the school's most popular teacher on my first day."

Jules could feel the flaming heat colouring her cheeks, but she wasn't sure whether it was from what Gethin had just seen, or the embarrassment of his compliment.

"I don't know who told you that," she said. "But I can promise you they're exaggerating."

"They all sounded pretty convincing. But that's beside the point. Is there anything I can do to help?"

Jules swallowed as she tried to work out how to answer. Obviously, telling the truth about why she was banging her head on the table was not an option. But saying there was nothing wrong, when her actions so clearly indicated otherwise, wasn't an option either. And it wasn't like there was anything she needed help with, which meant she either had to tell him she was merely in the middle of an existential crisis, or she had to make something up.

"Oh, it's just the new software system," she said. "You know how they are. They always take a bit of getting used to."

"Oh." Gethin's face lit up at this news. "Well, if that's your problem, I can absolutely help. I happened to oversee training on this exact system at my old school. Here, let me pull up a chair, and we can go through it together."

CHAPTER 8

By the time Jules headed home, her phone was alight with three missed calls from Nate. Only they weren't technically missed. Her phone had been sitting there, on her desk, right within arm's reach, when it had buzzed and she had let it ring. She had watched it, shifting around in her chair, until the buzzing finally stopped, and then thirty minutes later she had done it all again, though this time she had shut her phone in her drawer and switched it to silent. At least that way she could try to pretend it wasn't ringing. There was simply no way she could answer it. What would she say? Looking forward to our date. Can't be late though as I'm teaching your daughter about the Saxons the next morning?

Besides, she had more important things to think about than Nathaniel that day.

Under normal circumstances, Jules didn't like to accost Austin as soon as he'd got home from school. He needed time to relax and decompress from the stresses of the day, just like she did. But this wasn't a normal day. This was his first day at secondary school, and she wanted to know everything. With only a slight knock on his bedroom door, she stepped inside to find him collapsed on a beanbag with a book in his hand. She doubted there was a single eleven-year-old in the world who had a room as clean as Austin's, which was why she didn't get too annoyed when, as was often the case, he didn't look up when he saw her. She sat down on the chair at his desk and swivelled it around to face him.

"So, tell me all about it."

With his nose still lost in the pages, he offered her an exceptionally nonchalant shrug.

"It was good."

Jules waited for a more detailed or elaborate description. None came.

"Good? Just good?" she pressed.

"Fine. It was fine."

"Fine? Fine is even worse than good."

Finally, he lifted his head to look at her, before slipping a bookmark into the page and placing the book on the ground beside him.

"Sorry, I was just reading something. Yes, it was fine. Good. To be honest, I don't know why people make such a fuss about moving to secondary school. It really wasn't that big of a deal."

"Well, it is a big deal, to me at least. Now tell me about your day. What lessons did you have?"

Aware that Jules wasn't simply going to get up and leave, Austin shifted about into a more comfortable position on his beanbag.

"The morning was all admin really, getting our timetables, finding out what classes we were in, meeting our tutors, that type of thing."

"And what about your tutor? Who've you got? Are they nice?"

At this, Austin's face finally showed some animation. The casual nonchalance that he had been trying to display since Jules arrived – and probably would have got away with had Jules not known him so well – was replaced with a definite twinkle in his eyes.

"I've got Mrs Falkes. She's good. Old. A bit strict, but guess what?"

"What?" Jules had no idea where this conversation was going.

"She's the one who runs the school debate team. Awesome, right? And I asked her if we could use tutor time to practice debates ready for team try-outs. She said we could do that once a week, after she'd given our notices and things, but then I pointed out it was only four weeks to the try-outs and four practices and that wouldn't be enough to get us ready to compete against some of the older years, so she upped it to twice a week, and three times if we don't have assembly. Cool, right? Now I know for sure I'm going to get in."

A knot twisted in the pit of Jules's stomach. She knew for sure he was going to get in, too. Which meant she now had to scrape together every spare penny for this trip abroad. Only there weren't any spare pennies. She'd already had to ask Vicky to up her contribution to the household bills as they continued to rise and almost every product she bought from the supermarket was own brand, or in the yellow sticker, reduced pile.

There was always the option of tutoring, she thought. Parents had asked her more than once if she would help their children with extra maths or English and had always refused because she didn't want to spend any time away from Austin. But with him at secondary school now, maybe it could work. After all, there were plenty of after-school clubs he could be doing. And she could always have the students come to her house to ensure he wasn't left on his own. Maybe that would work.

"Mum? Are you okay?"

Jules blinked, bringing herself back to the moment.

"Sorry, yes, I'm fine. Just thinking about my baby boy all grown up."

He rolled his eyes in a typical teenager manner.

"Don't worry, I'll still be living here for years. But is there anything else you wanted? Only we've been set this book to read in English and I'd really like to finish it tonight."

"Tonight? They set you an entire book to read in a night?"

"No, they set us ten pages, but there's no point doing anything by halves, is there?"

Later, as she was clearing up after dinner, Jules stared at the string of messages she and Nate had exchanged. It was nights like this when she hated how Vicky had Oliver. With Austin tucked away upstairs, the house felt eerily quiet, and she could have done with another person to sound off to. Besides, the longer she was on her own, the more likely it was that her willpower would fail, and she'd message Nate back, and she desperately didn't want that. What she needed was a group of people she could talk to who would stop her from doing anything stupid. And luckily, she had one ready and waiting.

She picked up her phone and dialled the number.

"Hello?"

"Hey, it's me," Jules said. "I need to talk.'

CHAPTER 9

It took fifteen minutes to gather a group of girls from the book club to come to her aid. Not for a second had Jules thought that they would all be able to make it. Eunice was in her eighties and though she was still getting out and about with no issues, her great-nephew, could be a little overbearing, and was unlikely to let her wander to the other side of Maldon in the evening.

Dee messaged back straight away to say that she had a dinner party that night, which was obviously fine and Jules only really needed one other person to talk things over with. Yet she ended up with far more.

Maria, Nina, Gemma, Sophie, and Fleur all turned up at her door, some with wine, some with chocolate, and one with a large tub of ice cream, which Jules put straight into the freezer. Technically speaking, Fleur disrupted the ethos of the Lonely Hearts Book Club, given that she was now in a relationship with Eunice's overbearing great-nephew, Henry, but she had been single when she joined, so they all let it slide. Besides, deep down, they knew that was what they all wanted; to not be a lonely heart anymore. Given how Henry had been a self-proclaimed bachelor when they met, and Fleur had openly despised him, she was living proof that it was never too late to meet your one.

When all the drinks were poured, they sat around in the living room, waiting for Jules to recount the events of the last three days to them. Or at least, all the events that involved Nate.

"So, this is the man you met on Friday night? The one we couldn't tear you away from?" Sophie said, topping up her and Maria's glasses with wine as she spoke. All the others, Jules included, had opted for soft drinks, though she thought that might well change depending on the outcome of these conversations.

"You didn't try very hard to tear me away. You just stood and watched and giggled," Jules said defensively. "But yes, it's him."

"And she kissed him!" Sophie lifted her hands excitedly while she looked at the others as she spoke. "It was really romantic, too. All the twinkling lights and everything."

Jules groaned inwardly. The last thing she needed was Sophie reminding her of just how perfect that kiss had been. How perfect he had been.

"It's not just that we kissed, though. We spoke for hours on the phone afterwards. And we were going to meet up for dinner later in the week, but now I don't think I should. In fact, I know I shouldn't, right? I can't meet up for a drink with him. I teach his daughter. And he's married."

"You said he was separated," Gemma countered. Jules took a deep breath in.

"What does that even mean? It's not divorced, is it? And his wife seems to think it's just a bump in the road and that they'll get back together. She's still wearing all her rings and everything. It can't be that serious a separation if she's wearing her wedding ring, can it?"

Her eyes scanned the room as she waited for one of the girls to offer her some pearl of wisdom that she hadn't thought of, but everyone was remaining tight-lipped.

"This is why we need Graham here," Sophie said, breaking the silence. "We need a male perspective."

A few throats cleared, but no one said anything. Graham was as unlucky in love as the rest of them, only his situation was even more painful to watch, given how clearly he doted on Sophie. How she couldn't see it, nobody knew, but considering he hadn't even managed to ask Sophie out for a drink, when he sat next to her for several hours a week, Jules seriously doubted that his perspective would be any better than the rest of theirs.

"Let's ignore the married part for a second," Nina said, leaning forward in her seat. "If he was completely single. Not married, no other woman on the scene. Then would you still feel comfortable dating him? Given that he's a parent of one of your students."

The knots that had been pestering Jules all day reached a new level. It was a question she probably should have asked herself from the very beginning of this debacle, but she hadn't, most likely because she already knew the answer.

"I don't think I would, no."

"Then you have your answer."

Silence filled the room. A silence in which she could feel her friends' hearts aching for her, almost as much as her own. How was this possible? For a split second she had allowed herself to believe in happy ever afters, and maybe it hadn't been so dramatic as love at first sight, but there had definitely been a lot of emotions after just a couple of days. And now she was forced to give it all up before even finding out if this could be something real.

"I think you need to speak to him, though. Clear the air," Maria said. "You're going to have to see him at things like parents' evening, aren't you? You don't want that to be awkward."

"I agree," Fleur said. "Make sure he knows where the boundaries are. That he's not to message you from now on or anything."

Jules nodded. It was a good point. If she didn't do something, she would dread every parents' evening and every email home for the rest of the year. Even pick-ups on the school gate would be toe-curlingly embarrassing. For her peace of mind, she needed to make sure this thing was packed up fully, with no chance of misunderstanding.

"Yes, you're right. I'll end things completely. Tell him nothing is ever going to happen. It might just have to be a telephone conversation, though. Vicky's not back until Friday, and I don't want to leave Austin on his own."

At this, she was met by a sea of raised eyebrows.

"What?" she said.

"It's fine," Fleur piped up from her place on the edge of the room. "I don't mind babysitting Austin for a couple of hours if you want to see Nate and call things off that way. I'm only just up the road. You could go see him tomorrow. Or tonight, even. Why don't you go tonight? We can stay here."

Jules wanted to refuse. She wanted to go back to the morning and pretend the day had never happened, but it didn't matter how much she wished for it, that would never happen. And so, with a deep breath in, she reached over, picked up Sophie's wine glass and downed the lot.

"You're right," she said. "I'll message him now.'

CHAPTER 10

If Jules was to back out and leave, then this was the last moment to do it. Nate was there, waving from the water, the blue sail of his boat flapping lazily in the breeze. If she turned around and headed back now, there was no chance of him being able to follow her. But now that she was looking at him, she didn't know if she could leave. The girls had made her message him the night before, while they were still there, to arrange a time to meet. In less than a minute, Nate had pinged a message back. He was free the following evening. Could they meet by the water? So now Jules was standing on the sea wall, waving at Nate on his yacht, while Fleur was at her house, listening to Austin discuss the plight of the Rohingyas in Myanmar.

As Jules gazed across the water, her stomach flipped over itself repeatedly.

This was the Nate she had met. The Nate with the broad smile and wide eyes. The one that had put her so at ease, she'd felt like she'd known him for months after only one meeting. It was almost impossible to believe it was the same sour-faced parent she had met at the school. This was her Nate. She immediately quashed the thought. He wasn't her Nate. He was married, parent Nate, and she had come here to tell him things were over between them.

With the expertise of someone who had been sailing their whole life, he brought the boat close to the seawall where Jules was standing.

"I thought it would give us a bit more privacy," he said, needing to shout just a fraction to make himself heard. "There's a jetty, just down the way. If you walk there, I'll meet you and you can come aboard."

"Okay." Jules was too stunned by the situation to even consider how to respond, although as she watched Nate sail in the direction he had pointed, a fresh fear gripped her.

Despite growing up in Maldon, where so many people sailed, Jules had never been one for boats. She had been out on them before – one of her school friends had spent her sixteenth birthday on a narrowboat in nearby Heybridge, there was even a boat that was converted into a café for the summer, but unlike so many school children, her parents had never been particularly bothered about being on the water, and though she had often thought she might find some enjoyment relaxing out under the sun with the waves lapping on the hull, the idea of paying for sailing lessons, when she was struggling to cover the cost of new school shoes every time Austin out grew an old pair, wasn't viable.

For a second longer, she remained where she was. Transfixed by the sight of the sail as it came to a halt by a small jetty. With what was as close to a jog as Jules did, she headed to the jetty. There, perched with a rope in his hand, was Nate.

"Here, climb on. It's pretty steady. Just watch your footing." He offered out his hand to Jules, but rather than taking it, she shuffled back by a fraction.

"I didn't come down here to go for a sail. I came down here to talk to you."

"I know, and this way we won't get interrupted at all." He tipped his head to the side, his eyes twinkling the same way they had before he kissed her. "So, are you going to come on board or not?"

Jules stared at his hand. Now that she knew about it, she thought she could see a faint tan line on his ring finger where his wedding band had been. Though it could easily have been her imagination.

"You know, it's not as easy holding this thing in place as you think," Nate pressed. Before she could second-guess herself, Jules reached out and stepped on board.

She planted one foot, then another into the boat, keeping a close eye on the large metal bar to which the sail was attached. The boom? Was that what it was called? Whatever it was, she felt certain it was going to swing across and strike her any minute.

"Just give me a second to get us out onto the water, then we can talk," Nate said, and turned his attention to the series of ropes. With nothing to do but watch him, Jules took a seat, then slouched a little further down into the space, just to make sure her head was safe.

In less than a minute, the sail was taut in the wind, and the boat swiftly moved them away from the wooden jetty. Light, feathery clouds were thickening in the sky and it was only as Jules looked out over the water that she noticed how they were at high tide; the muddy marshland that could so frequently surround the waters was now filled and glistening.

"Okay, we should be good." His voice brought Jules's attention away from the river and back to Nate. Or, more importantly, the fact that she was alone on a boat with him.

With the rope still in his hand, he took a seat next to her.

His close presence was all it took for her pulse to rise. Swallowing back the heat that flooded her cheeks, she shifted herself away from him.

"You didn't mention you sailed," she said eventually.

"No, that's because we weren't talking about work, remember? It would've saved us an awkward moment if we had."

They had barely been alone for three minutes, and Jules found herself disappointed he had already mentioned the elephant in the room. But what else did she expect? It was why she'd come there. And now that he'd addressed the situation, she should probably wrap things up. But if she did that, ended it then and there, there would be nothing left for them to talk about, and this evening would be over and she wasn't quite ready. And so she tried to delay the moment a little longer.

"So you work with boats?" she said.

"I do. And you work as a primary school teacher. At my daughter's school."

The knot inside her tightened. There was no avoiding it now. He had brought it up twice, meaning that he wanted to talk about it.

Jules swallowed back the lump that was forcing its way up her throat. This was good, she reminded herself. Addressing the situation was what she wanted to do, or what she was supposed to want to do. So why was it so hard?

She gazed back out at the water, where the gentle ripples held her attention a moment longer, before she turned back to face Nate.

"You have a wife," she said.

"We're separated."

"She doesn't seem to think that."

"She's the reason we're separated. Please, I don't know what she said to you after she made me leave, but I can guess.

Something about a rough patch? About a temporary situation? It's not temporary. She cheated on me. Multiple times."

Perhaps it was a lie, she thought. After all, it sounded like the type of thing someone would say to make you feel sorry for them, but she saw the way his jaw clenched, and how the twinkle in his eye had all but evaporated.

"I'm so sorry."

Nate shrugged before tugging on the mainsail and shifting their path in the water. "You'd think I'd grow used to it. I kind of did. And the thing is, I'd almost felt like that was how relationships were meant to be. A constant back and forth power struggle."

"But you both moved down here together?" Jules said. After all, if he was that keen on a separation, why would he have packed them up and made them move? That sounded far more like someone who was looking for a fresh start.

"No. I got the job before I found out about the last affair. We were meant to be moving together, but for obvious reasons, the last thing I wanted was to play happy families. That's why I had to sort out somewhere else to live. Evie and Flick have taken the house we originally sorted."

"So she followed you down here, even though you wanted to separate?" Jules wanted to make sure she was following everything correctly.

"This job was too good for me to pass over, Flick knows that. And she realised that I'd never leave Evie. So either she moved too, or she had one hell of a battle on her hands. One she probably wouldn't win. Besides, I think she hoped that this show of goodwill, moving here with me, would be enough for me to consider the state of our relationship."

"Has it been? Packing up and moving is a pretty sure sign of someone's feelings, isn't it?"

"No. Not even close."

His voice didn't waver even slightly as he said this, yet Jules couldn't meet his eye. With his single spare hand, he reached across and took hers.

"Jules, we haven't done anything wrong. I am separated from my wife. I promise. I can show you the emails on my phone that I've written to this divorce lawyer I found in town here, if you don't believe me." He pulled his phone out of his pocket and started swiping around on the screen, but Jules put her hand out to stop him.

"It's not just about Flick. Not entirely. It's about Evie too. She's starting over in a strange town, with no one she knows, and she shouldn't have to deal with her teacher dating her father. Ignoring the fact that I don't even think I'm allowed to do that, I don't think I should."

"Your job can't dictate your dating life, surely?" Nate spoke with near disgust. "Besides, we did nothing wrong. We met before you even knew I was a parent at your school."

"You think school is going to believe that? Do you think Flick is going to believe that?"

He pressed his lips together tightly in a line. Somehow, the moodiness made him look even more adorable. Her heart pounded in her chest. If she could have run away, she would have. Just to get away from the overwhelming urge to wrap her arms around him and kiss him again. But short of diving into the water, there was nowhere she could go. She was stuck.

"Jules, this is ridiculous. I know it is." Nate's hand was on hers again. "But there's something here. Something real. I felt it the first time I saw you, and I know you felt it too." His voice was barely a whisper above the waves. "All I've been thinking about since I saw you in the classroom was how much I want to kiss you again. How I have to kiss you again."

Her heart was pounding now. Her pulse drumming so

hard she was amazed he couldn't hear it. And it would be so easy. So easy to just shift forward and kiss his lips. "Nate, this doesn't help. I think you should take me back now."

He nodded, although his head moved closer to hers by just a fraction, and she still couldn't bring herself to move away.

"Of course. Of course I will." She could feel his breath on her cheek. "But is that before or after I kiss you?'

CHAPTER 11

Jules slept even worse than she had the previous night and that was saying something. Once again, she was plagued with school-related nightmares, although rather than consisting of forgetting how to teach, or being asked to do an entire school assembly on some ridiculous topic, like nanophysics or how to lay turf, she was plagued by images of Nate appearing in her class. Nate and Flick, Nate and Dawn Dowling, the head. Nate and Gethin. It didn't matter who he was there with. Each of the dreams had the same ending – they had busted her for kissing a student's parent and there would be consequences.

At four o'clock, when she heard the front door open, she gave up. Fetching her dressing gown from the back of the door, she headed downstairs, wide awake, but grateful to finally have someone to talk to.

"What are you doing up?" Vicky said. She was still dressed in her scrubs, and her hair that had been in a topknot was almost entirely splayed out across her face.

"What are you doing here? I thought you were staying at Oliver's."

"I was, but he's had to head up to Scotland for a few days. Anyway, I'm the one who asked first. Why are you up this early? Please don't tell me you're working."

Jules took a deep breath in before she spoke. "We kissed. Again."

"We… as in?"

"Me and Nate."

Given the solemnity with which Jules had relayed this news, she expected Vicky to be somewhat sympathetic. Or perhaps even critical. Instead, a wide grin broke across her face.

"This is amazing. When? How? Why are you looking so miserable? Oh god, was he a terrible kisser? I'm so sorry, that's crap."

With no comment, they moved into the living room, where Vicky flopped onto the sofa. Jules looked at the clock on the wall. She normally got up at five-thirty; that gave her time to do a home exercise video, and make both her and Austin packed lunches, along with catching up on any last-minute planning or marking that needed to happen before Austin woke up and the day started for real.

"No, he's not a terrible kisser. He was an amazing kisser." She dropped onto the sofa beside Vicky and let her mind wander back to the moment on the boat. Even the memory was enough to send a shiver down her spine. It was early evening, the sun was setting, and the clouds cast shifting shadows on the shallows. She had closed her eyes, and waited, her heart battering inside her chest, her body so nervous that goosebumps lifted her skin. But she didn't move. She needed him to be the one to kiss her. And he did. With his hand pressed against her cheek, he lowered his lips to hers. A thousand fireworks exploded within her, and when he finally broke away, she found her eyes were still closed as the faint whispers of a sigh drifted from her lips.

And then she had turned away and faced the water, so he couldn't see the tears in her eyes as she said, "This can't happen again."

"I don't get it. If he's a great kisser and you still like the guy, what's the problem?" Vicky's voice brought Jules back into the room.

Jules frowned.

"Didn't you read the messages I've been sending you for the last two days? He's married. Well, separated, and he has a child in my class?"

"What?" Vicky's eyes bulged. "What? No. I mean, I saw the messages, but I thought they were you panicking about Austin being at secondary school, so I ignored them. Crap friend alert. Wow, okay, what's happened? Tell me everything."

Blowing out a deep sigh, Jules stood back up. "Fine, but I'm going to need to make a cup of tea."

Once again, Jules sat in her living room, reciting the incident with Nate and Flick, now with the extra addition of heading out on the boat and kissing him for a second time.

"I met him to tell him things were over." She let out an exasperated sigh as she spoke. "But then he was there with his boat, telling me to get on board. And I told him it couldn't happen. I told him it couldn't. But..."

"But you kissed again." Leaning forward, Vicky rested her hands on her chin, enquiringly. "So he's definitely separated?"

"He said I could see the emails he sent to his divorce lawyer."

"I'd say that's pretty concrete, wouldn't you?"

"I guess so. And he said they were separated in front of his daughter too. I guess you wouldn't do that unless you genuinely meant it."

"And you like each other, and you met him before you even knew he had a child at the school."

"That's what he said, but you know how important my job is to me."

It was more than just that. It was what being in her job meant. After everything she had gone through growing up, with all the neighbours and school colleagues assuming she'd never amount to anything, now the fact she worked in the most prestigious prep school in the town was a sign that she had made it. That the rumour mills and gossips hadn't beaten her down. The last thing she wanted was to be at the centre of another scandal, and whether she liked it or not, she and Nate dating would be exactly that.

"It doesn't matter anyway," she said, grabbing a cushion from behind her and holding it against her chest. "It's over now."

"Over over?"

"I told him. After we kissed, I told him that was it."

"And what did he say to that?"

Jules thought back to the moment. The way his fingers stayed interlocked with hers, and how his eyes had bored so deeply into hers it made her dizzy. And then, with his lips still by her ear, he'd whispered. *"I don't think it's going to be as easy as you want to pretend."*

"It doesn't matter what he said." Jules straightened her back, trying to erase the memory from her mind. "It's my decision, and I've made it.'

CHAPTER 12

The next two days were too busy for Jules to contemplate dating anyone, with barely a minute to breathe, let alone sit down for a proper meal, or meet someone for a drink. But even that lack of time didn't stop her from thinking about Nate. It was almost impossible, given that she saw his daughter for seven hours a day.

Evie was truly delightful. While she had come across as somewhat shy during her first day, by the end of Thursday, she had been offering answers to almost every question they asked. Like she said, she was very into English, with a vocabulary that was well above the average in the class. Her use of problem solving in maths was incredibly strong, and her artwork was some of the best Jules had seen from someone in her year. At least, Jules considered, she wouldn't need to ring home saying that Evie needed extra help. That was something, at least.

"Thank you, Miss Chard," Evie said, as she queued up to leave the classroom at the end of the day. Thankfully, Jules's duties that term were at break time, monitoring the children while they were at play. Normally, it wasn't her favourite duty time. She'd much rather have a morning or afternoon on the gate, welcoming or dismissing the students to and from school. But this year that would have been a disaster. She couldn't have imagined anything worse than starting her day seeing Nate's perfect smile glittering at her from the other side of the school gates. Or Flick in all her perfection flashing her diamonds. When next term came around, Jules was already planning on swapping duties to maintain the same ones again. Anything to limit her exposure to Nate.

Thursday afternoon was staff meeting time. Frances always said that the management team picked that day deliberately, to ensure people didn't get too excited about the upcoming weekend too soon, seemingly forgetting that for the best part of a decade, she had been at the top level of the management team. That was before she'd begun her will-she-won't-she retire charade.

Rather than taking place in the staffroom, it took place in the main school hall, where benches, which were only fractionally higher than the tiny chairs, were placed out for the teachers to sit on. During her very first meeting at the school, Frances had accosted Jules in the doorway, told her to go straight back to her classroom and fetch a cushion to sit on. It was a habit she stuck to even now.

Several people had slots to speak during the meeting, including Gorgeous Gethin, as several of the other staff had already nicknamed him. With his role in pastoral and children's well-being, he repeated the same things that they heard every year, this time just in a Welsh accent, after which it was back to Dawn, the headteacher.

"I know that we haven't even finished our first week yet,

but I do want us to be looking ahead," she said. Dawn Dowling was, quite possibly, the smallest headteacher in history, barely reaching five feet, and a complete contrast to the towering Frances, who had done the role before her, but the parents loved her, and the teachers were generally in agreement with her suggestions too. "It's a very busy term. Key Stage 1 are doing their first Parents' Assembly in only three weeks' time, and there is the Year 1 and 2 zoo trip before half term. Not to mention we'll have the whole play, and the Year 4 and 5 residential trip to Danbury lakes."

Jules stopped listening at the mention of the school play. Last year, her only role had been ensuring the children were wearing the right costumes and following the actions which she performed with exaggerated arm movements at the back of the room. Hopefully, she would get the same type of role this year.

"Please try to get parents involved as much as possible. We are going to need help with all the performances and not just on the actual days. Mrs Keegan has some fantastic ideas about set design, so we'll need all hands on deck to make those happen. And let's not forget we'll need chaperones for all the trips, too. It's never too late to get parents to sign up, so start talking to them about it now."

For the rest of the meeting, Jules daydreamed about exactly how these parent events would go with her and Nate. She could only assume that he would leave it to Flick. It wouldn't be ideal. After all, she had kissed the woman's husband twice, once when she had known about his situation. But it would still be better than having to be with Nate.

When the meeting was over, she picked up her cushion from her spot on the bench and stretched out the cramps in her legs.

"Time for a Chinese takeaway," Frances said.

"Sounds good. Time to see what I have in the freezer," Jules replied, already aware that she wouldn't find much. That was another thing. Austin was now rapidly eating them out of house and home. What he had once considered a full meal he now devoured as nothing more than a light snack, so every meal she gave him had to be substantial. Hopefully, she had a couple of jacket potatoes at the back of a cupboard somewhere. They would fill him up.

"Jules, do you have a second?"

Jules jolted back into the moment, and the realisation she was still at school. There, looking directly at her, was a tall woman with piercing blue eyes.

"Amanda? Yes, sorry, of course."

Amanda was the school secretary and the only person, other than Frances, to have been at the school for over twenty years. Her near white hair was accented with massive pink dangly earrings.

"I just had a telephone call from one of your parents. They want to have a chat."

Jules held in the internal sigh. She had hoped to get back home early, in case she needed to head to the shops. Phone calls could last anywhere between five and forty minutes.

"Okay, I'll call them straight back," she said, hoping it would be quick.

"They'd rather meet you in person, apparently. Would you be able to spare ten minutes before class starts tomorrow?"

Jules took a moment to mentally scan through her next day. The children had English, then maths, both of which were planned. Then after break it was art. As far as days went, it was a nice and relaxed one.

"Yes, that's fine. I can do then."

"Fantastic. I'll ring them back now and let them know."

It was only when Amanda turned away that Jules realised she didn't know who she was meeting.

"Amanda, which parents is it?"

"Sorry." Amanda smiled broadly. It was the perfect smile to welcome students into the school. It was no wonder everyone loved her. "I should have said. It's Felicity Campbell. Evie's mother.'

CHAPTER 13

All the way back home, the fear of being discovered clawed at Jules's insides, gnawing away at her composure. She could imagine all too well the various scenarios of discovery – perhaps Flick had seen the messages on Nate's phone or witnessed the intimate moment on his boat. Perhaps someone had mentioned the kissing outside the pub, before Jules even knew who he was, or maybe Nate had just buckled and confessed to what they'd done. There was the slight chance that this was merely a parent-teacher meeting to discuss Evie's progress, but that seemed too optimistic.

Fortunately, when she arrived home, a distraction came in the form of an unusually lively Austin.

"Guess what, Mum?"

"Hi Mum, how was your day?" Jules mocked as Austin continued to bounce around.

"I found the sport I want to do."

"Really, that's great," she responded, and genuinely meant it. Jules never needed to worry about Austin being sociable; he had a great group of friends, most of whom he would see almost every weekend. But they would spend their time indoors. If they weren't on computer games, then they were building models out of Lego or Technic or rebuilding the circuit board of a 1980s computer that Jules had picked up at a car boot sale for him. She couldn't remember the last time he had played outside, be it football, or den building, unless it was to set off the rockets he was given as part of a science experiment gift pack from Vicky. She had tried skateboards and scooters, and even took him over to a Parkour centre in Witham once. Though, to be fair, it was her who wasn't keen on him carrying on with that; there were only so many times you could watch your only child jump from an eight-foot box and not panic.

"What is it?" she asked. "And where is it? I know you think you're old enough, but I really don't want you getting the bus to Chelmsford on your own yet."

"It's fine, Mum, it's in Maldon. Well, Heybridge, but it's close, and it's on Saturday, meaning I'll be out of your hair for a couple of hours in the morning."

"That does sound good. Are you going to tell me what it is or not?"

"Sailing."

"Sailing?"

"Yup." His face was glowing with a broad grin that lit his eyes. "It's perfect. Universities love it if you have a sport on your applications, and this one requires actual skill. Like scientific skills. I need to consider the velocity of the water and the wind, the tension in the sails. I've already started researching the science of it, and honestly, some of the polymers they use to make boats nowadays are incredible." The grin was even wider now, taking up over half of his face. Normally, it was the type of expression that would make Jules's heart leap and fill her with lightness, but today it sat there like a dead weight, as she knew she had to be the one to remove it.

"Austin, sailing is expensive. It's not just the boats, but the lessons. Life jackets. All the gear. I'm really sorry, I can't stretch to that at the minute. Perhaps if I get one of the Head of Key Stage jobs next year, we can look again, but we'll have to put a pin in it until then. I'm really sorry."

It wasn't the first time in their lives she had had to tell Austin they couldn't do something because of money. It had been hard when he was little, and Father Christmas was bringing the other children animatronic dinosaurs or the latest games console and he was getting new pyjamas or chocolate selection packs. But he was a bright child, and over the last couple of years had only ever asked for things that he really wanted. Which was what made this even worse. Despite this, his smile remained fixed on his face.

"That's the thing, Mum, it's free."

"Free?"

"Free sailing lessons?"

"Yup, look." He handed her a form, which she quickly scanned. A twelve-week free sailing school course, offered by one of the local yacht clubs.

"Wow, that sounds great, buddy, but it's still only twelve weeks. After that, they're expecting you to pay and I still won't have the money for you to continue. What happens if you really love it and you have to stop?"

His eyes twinkled with mischief. "I've already thought about that. If I really like it, and I'm really good at it, then hopefully someone will take me on as a member of their crew. Teach me that way. Or I could volunteer at the club, you know, hanging up life jackets, that type of thing, and maybe they'd throw a couple of lessons my way for free."

"You really have thought this through, haven't you?" Jules said, half wondering why she had doubted her son.

"Yes, I have. There's only one problem."

"What's that?"

"It's first come, first served. So can you sign the letter now, please, and send an email, just in case? And I'll need to be at school a bit early tomorrow just to make sure I'm there first."

Jules's face was now matching Austin's with a smile. It didn't matter what was going on outside their four walls, somehow, inside this house he always made her smile.

"Sure, I can do that." Jules dropped the letter onto the table, grabbed a pen from the pot on the side, and signed the letter. "I guess it's an early morning for both of us," she said.

THE NEXT MORNING, Austin was already eating breakfast and waiting when Jules came down for her morning yoga in front of the television.

"Wow, you really are serious about this?"

"Sure I am. And guess what? James is trying to get on it too. We're going to be the first two, waiting for when they open the school gates. Then we can share lifts. Or get the bus to Heybridge together."

"Sounds perfect."

Unlike Austin, Jules was not in a hurry to get to school that morning. In fact, she was almost in an anti-hurry. For a weak-willed moment, she considered calling in sick only to realise that was ridiculous. She was meeting with a parent, that was all. She had met with hundreds of them in her career, and this was going to be no different. That was what she tried to convince herself as she picked out an outfit that was slightly newer than most of the clothes in her wardrobe and took a little extra time doing her makeup.

After that, there was no way she could avoid it any longer. She needed to get to school.

Tension riddled Jules's shoulders and neck as she sat in her classroom and waited. Normally, she would fetch herself a cup of tea, but that morning she'd already drunk two cups of coffee before she'd even arrived at school, and more caffeine didn't seem like a good idea. So, instead, she paced her classroom, straightening chairs and fixing displays that didn't need to be fixed. After what felt like an eternity, at seven-fifty, there was a knock on her door.

Adrenaline surged through her as she gritted her teeth and turned towards the door.

Somehow, Flick looked even more immaculate than she had before, her light strawberry-rose hair perfectly matched with a dark green dress. On anyone else, the dress might have looked like a sack, but on Flick, it flowed straight down without a single crease.

"Flick – Ms Campbell," Jules corrected herself mid-sentence.

"Please, Flick is fine, although it is Mrs Campbell."

"Sorry, yes. Mrs Campbell. Flick."

Without waiting for an invitation, Flick strode into the room. Jules was amazed at how anyone could walk so elegantly in such high heels. She wouldn't have managed two steps without falling flat on her face. While Flick glided in, Jules moved to close the doors and she turned around. Flick was staring straight at her.

"I want to talk to you about my husband," she said.

CHAPTER 14

The heat was stifling, beads of perspiration budding on Jules's forehead and neck.

"You want to talk about your husband? Mr Campbell?" She choked the name out, trying to stifle the dizziness that was currently crippling her.

"Yes, can we sit?"

"Of course, yes, of course."

She was both lightheaded and nauseous, and no matter how much she tried to stop it, Jules knew was shaking. Trying to steady her steps, her brain whirred on overdrive. She would just apologise, she decided. That was the best thing she could do. Apologise, explain she hadn't known who Nate was when she met him. But what about the kiss on Tuesday night? How could she explain that? She had known exactly who he was then, and yet she had still got on a boat with him. To end things, she reminded herself. That was all.

"The thing you need to understand," Flick began, "Is that my husband is very busy at the minute. Very busy. As we mentioned in our last meeting, there are a couple of issues in our relationship that we are currently working through."

"You don't need to tell me." Jules was feeling more and more sick by the second. If Flick would just hurry up and confront her, then at least this facade would be over.

"I think it helps for you to understand the situation fully," Flick continued "Anyway, I won't go into too much detail, but his job is the reason we are here, and I know the stress he feels over ensuring Evie settles well at school is adding to the pressures on him. For that reason, I wondered if you could stop sending him any parental communications."

"Sorry?" Jules straightened her back a little. Over the last twelve hours, she had run through a dozen different scenarios of how this conversation might go, and none of them involved this. "I'm not sure I understand?"

"I don't want Nathaniel receiving any communication from the school. Not emails, not notifications on the app. Not telephone calls."

The words "telephone call" prickled on Jules's skin. Did Flick know that she and Nate had spoken on the phone? If she did, she was doing an incredible job of remaining calm about it.

"I know it might be unorthodox, but I think it would be best for our relationship if I simply try to remove some of the stress from him, you understand."

"And does Nate – Mr Campbell – want this too?"

The lip purse said everything Jules needed to know. Of course, Nate didn't have any idea. Flick continued, nonetheless. "He will benefit from this, believe me. That's what matters."

As subtly as she could, Jules took a deep breath in. She had dealt with some odd requests as a teacher before, including one parent who asked her to spend at least thirty minutes a day reading with their child and one who had asked her to check there were no pips in any of the oranges given at break as her child didn't like them. Frances even had one incident in Year 6 where the parents had come in and asked if they would encourage more use of social media with their child as all they wanted to do was sit and draw, but this – having one parent coming in and trying to sideline the other – was something she couldn't have imagined.

"I'm afraid that's a question for the administration staff rather than myself," Jules said, thankful that she could find a diplomatic answer that was also true. Flick's smile widened and not in a warming manner.

"I do understand that, but given how Nathaniel, utterly inappropriately I must add, announced our current marital difficulties to you, I thought you might be the one who could sort this for me. You know what these places are like. I've already seen messages asking us to help with set painting and school trips. I don't want him to feel obliged to do these things. Not when his time is already so precious."

Dipping her smile by a fraction, Flick leaned forward and lowered her voice, and when she spoke, it was almost as if she was talking to a friend over a glass of wine. "I'll level with you, Julia. It is Julia, isn't it?"

"Jules."

"Jules. Right. I know you don't get my situation, having never been married yourself, but the schoolyard can be a tough place for parents, especially when you're new. And even more so in a school like this. I want to make the best impression, I want Evie to make the best impression, and I think the smoother we can make this, the better it would be for us all."

Jules struggled to digest what she had just heard. This woman wanted Nate to be stripped of communication from the school because she didn't want the other parents to gossip about them? She knew all about gossip. She and Austin had been the brunt of it for years. She could sympathise, yes, but there was no way she could agree.

With a deep breath in, Jules sat back on her seat and spoke.

"First of all, I don't think you need to worry about Evie. I mean that genuinely. She was out in the playground all day yesterday with a group of girls from the class trying to skip. And when they came in from break, they were battling to sit next to her."

Flick's eyes glimmered with a smile.

"That is great to hear. Really fantastic."

"And as for the other part, we have several parental setups in this school – single-parent families, adoptive families, same-sex families – and every student and member of staff is entirely sympathetic and empathetic to difficulties that can come with any situation. As for the removal of Mr Campbell from the school's database for contact, I'm afraid I don't have anything to do with that. I don't even have access to edit the school records and data. What I would suggest is that you talk to Nate—" Jules stuttered. "Mr Campbell, about this and find out if it's what he wants. Then contact the school office afterwards and they'll be happy to oblige."

The smile that had been so expertly fixed to Flick's face faltered for just a second as her eyes narrowed on Jules. The slip with the name had done it, Jules thought. This was where she was going to pounce. Instead, she stood up and straightened her dress.

"Well, that is disappointing," she said, then without another word, stood up and turned towards the door.

CHAPTER 15

The rest of Friday went by in a mad daze. After the morning classes, there was an afternoon assembly and show and tell, neither of which Jules could concentrate through. All she could do was go over the conversation in her head again and again. Would Flick really have said those things about Nate to her if she knew something happened between them? Maybe talking about Nate had been a way to make it clear that she was very much still a part of his life and knew what the two of them had been up to. It was certainly a more subtle way to make Jules steer clear than yelling at her outright. Not that Jules needed anyone telling her that staying away from Nate was the right thing to do. She knew it was.

After the kiss on Tuesday night, Jules had told Nate that that was it. Contact between them needed to end. And he lasted all the way until Friday evening. She and Austin had curled up together on the sofa to watch a Friday night film.

"It is my choice," Austin insisted. "And we are watching this. I don't think documentaries even count as films."

"Of course they do. That's why I always choose documentaries when it's my turn," Jules protested.

"Really? I thought it was because you hated me."

She picked up a cushion, ready to throw it at her son, when the phone buzzed. Immediately, her eyes fell on the name of the screen.

"Is it weird that I miss talking to you already?" He had written. That was it.

Her stomach somersaulted over and over as her thoughts began to spiral. No, she couldn't reply, she told herself, only to stop and reconsider. Would a simple response really be that bad? After all, as ridiculous as it was, she missed him, too. But that had to be her imagination, didn't it? After all, how could you miss someone you barely even knew? With a deep breath in, she turned her phone over and stayed strong. She would be fine. He would move on quick enough. There was no chance a man like him would be single for long.

THE FIRST AND last week of a school term were always the most exhausting, and as such, Jules was planning on spending her Saturday morning in bed. Because she was a single mum, lie-ins had been a no-go for nearly a decade, until eighteen months before, when Austin had made the switch from an obscenely early riser to a pre-teen far happier to see out the morning under the covers.

Now, on the odd occasion that he woke up before Jules, he would make a cup of tea and toast that he would bring into her room at half past ten, at which point they would sit together for another half an hour, watching videos of cats on her phone, before finally forcing themselves up to face the day. Which was why, at 8 a.m. when Austin bounded into her room, Jules assumed there must be something wrong.

"What are you doing?" she said, as he jumped onto the bed next to her. "Why are you up so early?"

"Why do you think? Sailing." Still groggy with sleep, Jules rubbed her eyes.

"What do you mean, sailing? You only put the letter in yesterday."

"Exactly. And it was only the first twelve that got selected. We got told then and there. We need to be down at the club by nine-thirty." He paused. "I can go by myself if it's easier. But I'll need to get the bus."

There was something in his voice that caused Jules to open her eyes fully. Sitting up, she looked at her son, who was wide-eyed, staring straight at her. So often she'd found herself caught short and scared by how quickly time had gone and how grown up he now was, but then there were other times, like then, when she knew in his voice, that he wanted her to come with him. No matter how old he was, he would always be her baby boy.

"Fine, but you need to go and make me a coffee," she said, stretching out so much that she deliberately pushed him off the edge of the bed.

"Hey!" He grabbed a pillow from the end of the bed, lifting it high as if he were going to bring it down on her.

"Remind me again, who had to give you permission to join this sailing activity?"

Immediately, Austin dropped the pillow.

"One cup of strong coffee coming up," he said.

THE AIR WAS full of the briny aroma of the estuary as they walked towards the water. The yacht club the school had partnered with for the sailing was in Heybridge, a short drive from the centre of Maldon, and was one of the places that she and Austin had gone kayaking in the summer. There were pubs and coffee shops along with an open green where people could sit and have a picnic, while a tidal lock placed at the mouth of the estuary allowed access between the river and the canals.

The crowds that had flocked there during the holidays were much depleted and as she stepped out of the car, Jules allowed herself a moment to bask in the sounds and aromas of the place.

The water lapped leisurely; its gentle rhythm accompanied by the soft chimes of ropes knocking against boat masts. This peacefulness was one of the things Julie loved about living by the water. A walk by the river was normally enough to lessen even the most stubborn tension from work and make her see all the good things about the place she lived, although, as her eyes fell on a sailboat, her stomach turned and she couldn't help but think of the last time she was on one. Or more importantly, who she was on one with.

"You okay, Mum? You're looking all dazed and weird?"

Jules snapped back into the moment.

"Sorry, yes. I'm fine. So, do you know where you're heading?"

"I've got to go down there." He pointed to a jetty where several small boats were moored. Already waiting alone was a tall boy with bright blonde hair who was waving furiously at them. Austin turned back to his mum. Clearly desperate to get moving. "I think they said there's a room inside the parents can wait in if you want to? And I know James's dad said he was going to stay."

"I guess that's probably the best thing. Do you know how long you're going to be?" If she thought about it properly, Jules would've brought some of her marking with her, but there didn't seem to be much point heading back. Still, she knew for next time.

"I think it's just an hour."

"Okay, well I'll go inside and wait then. Just make sure you get a life jacket that fits properly."

"Mum."

"What, you wanted me here." She pulled him forward and planted a kiss on his forehead, before turning him by the shoulders and letting him run off to join his friend.

There were plenty of yacht clubs in Maldon, and the surrounding towns, like Burnham and Fambridge. But Jules had never been a member at any. Still, she'd been inside the clubs often enough for things like weddings and Christenings. She doubted the members there had to worry about rising electricity or food costs like she did. A nervousness rose in her as she cast one more glance back at Austin, who had now joined his friend, and stepped through the large wooden doors and into the bar area.

A series of wooden tables were positioned flush to the window, offering a perfect view of the river outside, while a full bar was currently being restocked by an exhausted looking young man who may or may not have been home after a night out, judging by his hair and choice of clothing.

Three of the tables were already occupied, and it took Jules less than thirty seconds to work out where she was going to sit. Austin had been all the way through primary school with James, and so, unsurprisingly, she knew his father, Martin, fairly well. So when Jules saw him sitting there at the table with one other gentleman – whose back was facing her – she didn't hesitate to walk over. Their conversation was almost always the same – what clubs the boys were doing, how they were doing in lessons and so forth, but James was a good kid, and it would be nice to hear how his start of secondary had gone.

"Jules, I heard Austin was doing this too." Martin stood up and gestured to one of the free chairs opposite him. "Come, join us. This gentleman here is one of the generous sponsors."

At that moment, Jules could only see the back of his head, yet something corkscrewed within her. Something about his posture, and the slight waves to his hair. Even before he began to turn around, Jules knew who she was going to see. Still the disbelief hitched in her voice as he finally faced her.

"Nate?'

CHAPTER 16

For a split second, Jules stood there, staring like a fool. It had been bad enough that he had caught her off guard in the classroom, but twice in one week was absolutely ridiculous.

"Jules, come sit down," Martin continued to speak. "Nate, Jules's son and mine have been thick as thieves since primary school. Double trouble, that's what I call them. Not that they're any trouble, really. Either of them."

Jules's eyes remained locked on Nate, unable to move, and he appeared to be in exactly the same state. Staring. A second later, she snapped back to the moment and turned to Martin with a wide smile.

"I don't want to disturb you. You're obviously in the middle of a conversation."

"No, it's fine. It's fine. Did you say you know each other?" Martin said, with a nod towards Nate.

Jules's mouth was inexplicably dry, though she was doing better than Nate, who still hadn't looked away from her.

"Yes, well no. Sort of. Nate's daughter, Evie, is in my class this year."

"Oh, isn't this a coincidence? Well, Nate here was just telling me how he'd set this thing up for the local school. Making it accessible to everyone. Fabulous, isn't it?"

Jules felt her chin nodding, though she wasn't sure why. She looked back at Nate.

"You set this up? The sailing classes?"

Finally, Nate displayed some sign of life beyond blinking. He shifted slightly in his seat.

"Yes, and no. My business partner, the one I started the sailing school with, wanted to get the local schools involved. He's the one who put all the effort into it. I'm just here for support."

"He's being modest. Nate's the one who supplied the boats, too. Incredibly generous, isn't it? Take a seat," Martin encouraged again. Jules glanced around, internally praying she might recognise someone. Someone who she could make an excuse to go and speak to. But all the other people were packed tight around their tables, chatting away like cliques. In a last-ditch attempt, she looked at Nate pleadingly, hoping he might come up with a suitable excuse for why she couldn't stay.

Instead, what he said was, "Yes, come and join us."

There was no way out of it now, and she knew it. So, moving slowly, Jules slipped into the seat opposite Nate. The tension in the air was palpable, yet Martin seemed oblivious to it.

"So, how has Austin found the first week?" Martin said. "Let me guess, he's all about the debate team too? That's a pricey trip. I wonder if I might try to dissuade him for a couple of years, at least. Don't you think?"

"Yes," Jules agreed. "James is in the same tutor group too, right? Mrs Falkes?"

"Aye, he is." He turned his attention away from Jules. "So, you've got children too, Nate?"

"Just one, Evie. As I was saying, we've only just moved here, so it's a bit of an adjustment for her."

"She's doing wonderfully well," Jules piped in. "Really relaxed. She's got a brilliant sense of humour."

"That she has," Nate agreed. "She's quite the practical joker as well. Love her more than anything, but I wouldn't trust her as far as I could throw her."

Jules chuckled. "Does she get that from you?"

"It's possible."

"Well, I'm glad she's had a good start," Martin said, making Jules aware of his presence there. Somehow, once Nate had started talking, she'd forgotten it wasn't just the two of them together. Alone.

"And what about you?" Jules smiled at Nate, as if they were doing nothing more than attempting casual small talk. "You've just moved here, too. How are you finding the change?"

"Oh, it's had its ups and downs," Nate fixed his eyes solely on her, causing a bubbling to rush through the whole of her body. She desperately wanted him not to look at her like that. To not make it so obvious. Yet, any worries she had about Martin noticing evaporated when he jumped from his seat.

"Look, there's Hayley's mum. Have you met Hayley or her mum, Jules? They only moved to Maldon before the summer, like you, Nate. I should really go and say hello. You don't mind, do you?"

Jules smiled as a wave of relief rippled through her.

"No, I haven't. Not yet. You should say hello."

"We'll be fine," Nate added.

With a quick handshake to Nate and a nod to Jules, Martin disappeared to the other side of the bar, leaving Jules and Nate alone.

Silence descended. It wove its way around them, almost as if their lack of words could draw them closer to one another.

"I want to hold your hand so badly," Nate whispered, though he had barely finished when Jules cut across him.

"Does Flick know about us?"

"What?"

"Does Flick know about us? About what happened?"

His face crumpled into a mass of frown lines and for a second he looked far more like the Nate she had met in her classroom than the man she was used to.

"No. She doesn't know anything. I promise, I wouldn't say something to her without talking to you about it first. I'd never do that. Why do you ask?"

Jules pressed her lips together as she considered how to respond. Was there such a thing as teacher-parent confidentiality? She didn't think so, but it hardly felt professional to talk about Flick to Nate like this.

"She came to see me at school. For a meeting," she revealed, opting for a version of the truth that omitted any of the more sensitive elements. Nate, however, wasn't ready to let it go.

"She did? When?"

"Yesterday morning."

"Why?"

Jules regretted saying anything at all now. "She just wanted to check on how Evie was doing." She thought she had lied convincingly, but Nate was staring straight at her as if he could see through it all.

"Jules, what did she want?"

Still hesitating, Jules bit down on the inside of her cheek. "I'm not doing this, Nate. I'm not getting involved. Just talk to your wife about it."

"I hate it when you do that."

"Do what?"

"Say "my wife" like that. Jules, I've never lied to you." His hands were creeping across the table to hers, but she drew hers back and placed them on her lap. Still, it didn't stop him from leaning in closer, making her even more aware of just how amazing he smelt. "It's been over between Flick and me for a long time. She's having a harder time accepting it than she should. That's all it is. I promise, there's nothing between us."

There was so much sincerity in his voice, but it wasn't enough. He had obviously loved Flick enough to marry her and have a child with her at some point. Who was to say that moving to Maldon wasn't just the thing they needed to rekindle that love? Then where would that leave her, alone and heartbroken? No, it wouldn't happen. It couldn't. This, him being here, was just another test, and one she wouldn't fail a second time.

"I should probably meet Hayley's mother," Jules announced, rising to her feet.

"Jules, please don't."

"It's nice to see you again, Nate," she said, before turning on her heel and marching towards Martin, all while trying to ignore the prickling heat behind her eyes.

CHAPTER 17

All week, Austin couldn't stop talking about sailing. "The instructor said I was a natural. I was the first to tack. Did I tell you that?"

"You did. Several times."

"I think my plan is going to work. I think I was one of the strongest in the group. Don't you think? You were watching, weren't you?"

Jules avoided his gaze as she spoke. She had spent half the session scanning the bar, ensuring Nate wasn't close by, but at the same time half wishing he were. Even when she had looked out at the water, the children had been nothing more than coloured dots, on the larger white dots of the boats, and no matter how much she loved Austin, she had no idea which dot he was.

"I was watching, but I'll be honest, I have no idea whether you were good or not. It's not something I consider myself an expert in."

"Well, trust me, I'm good. But I won't ask about helping on a crew yet. Not till we've had a few more sessions."

A job at the yacht club Nate was a member of? She couldn't think of anything worse, yet she didn't need to mention that to Austin.

At school, Jules did a solid job of avoiding Nate and Flick. In fact, by the time the book club rolled around on Thursday, she had almost convinced herself that she'd stopped thinking about him. That was until the girls all started asking questions.

"So, you didn't know he was going to be at the sailing club at all?" Fleur asked. As the newest member of the club, it was her first time hosting, and, in true Fleur style, she had gone overboard. The dining table was covered in an abundance of mezze boards with meat, cheese, hummus, falafels. Not to mention dried fruits, fresh fruits, breads and various dips and crackers. She'd bought at least enough food to feed twice the number of people attending, although the thought made Jules slightly optimistic. Hopefully, there'd be plenty left over and Fleur would offer them doggy bags. That would cover Jules's lunch for the next day and maybe even a bit extra for Austin's lunch box. However, before that, they had the book club meeting. Not to mention the continual Nate discussions.

"No, I had no idea he was going to be there. I knew he sailed, obviously, but honestly, it was a real kick in the teeth. Every time I think I'm getting him out of my head, he appears. It's like the universe is playing with me."

"Or maybe the universe is giving you a sign that you're meant to be together?" Fleur countered. Sophie was quick to join in the romantic bandwagon.

"Maybe it's the universe telling you he's the one."

"If the universe is going to send me the one, I'd at least like him to be divorced first," Jules said.

Other than the interrogations, the book club was a good one. They were discussing a retelling based on a witch from

Ancient Greece, picked by Nina for its popularity at the library. Jules hadn't read historical fiction for a long time, but if this was the quality of the genre, she intended to read a lot more. She never thought she'd feel sympathy for a woman who turned men into pigs, but after closing the book on the final page, she felt nothing but that, with tears rolling down her cheeks. It was one of those wonderful meetings, where everyone agreed that the book was pure mastery, and by the end of the session, they were all vowing to put another of the author's books on their list.

When the evening ended – and as hoped, Fleur offered them all several Tupperware containers full of food – Jules hugged her host goodbye.

"Don't write Nate off straight away," Fleur said as she pulled away from Jules, yet still held her at arm's length. "The start of relationships aren't always easy. Take me and Henry. I could have kicked him to the kerb and given up on us half a dozen times. But if I'd done that, then I'd be missing out on so much."

"I know what you're saying, but Nate and I are not you and Henry, Fleur. You were both in very different situations. The only thing stopping Henry was his damn stubbornness. It's not so simple with me and Nate." Jules tried not to sound annoyed with her friend. After all, she knew she was only trying to help. But unfortunately, in her circumstances, realism and romanticism were very much at odds.

"Maybe it's as simple as you want to make it," Fleur said, before kissing Jules on the cheeks one more time.

AT SCHOOL THE NEXT MORNING, Jules arrived even earlier than usual. Austin's new friend, Hayley, lived on a different route, so his and James's walk to school involved a new detour. It was only a couple of extra minutes, but they still left ten minutes earlier, just to make sure. With Vicky having spent the night at Oliver's, Jules didn't see any point in hanging around. Unfortunately, the extra time she had hoped to gain in the classroom was immediately negated by Gethin Jones rapping his knuckles on her classroom door.

"Jules, do you have a spare minute?"

It would have been tempting to say no. She was busy with reading assessments and creative planning and could have done with another three hours in the day to get everything up to the standard she wanted. But knowing she couldn't say that to management, she offered the only acceptable reply.

"Yes, of course."

"Fabulous." Gethin's sartorial choices had been up for much discussion since he arrived at the school. The only other male teacher at St. Catherine's was Bob Johnson, a P.E. teacher, who lived in a sports shirt and shorts, regardless of whether it was summer or winter. The only times in the year he ever wore a shirt and tie were for parents' evening and the end-of-year assembly. The first time Jules had seen him in formal attire, she'd been so confused she hadn't even recognised him. As nice a guy as he was, Bob also had an irritating habit of falling asleep in the staffroom during break and lunch times and spreading himself out so that he took up at least three seats. But Gethin Jones didn't do shorts and T-shirts. Gethin Jones did waistcoats and pocket handkerchiefs.

"I hate to start the day like this, but I wanted to ask you a favour." He stepped into the room and closed the door behind him. Closed doors didn't make Jules feel confident. She was very much an open-door person.

"Oh, okay. Of course, ask away."

"I wondered if you'd be able to swap duties with me this

afternoon? I've seen you're down for playground duty at lunch break. I'm meant to be doing the gate at the end of the day, but a member of the board wants to meet me, and it's not really something I can say no to."

Jules knew exactly how not being able to say no to something felt. But doing the duty at the end of the day was exactly what she didn't want. Either Flick or Nate was going to be there and she would have to smile away at them, like she was just a happy teacher bidding her students farewell. Yes, she knew exactly what not being able to say no to something felt like.

"Is it just a one-day thing?" she said, trying to appear as diplomatic as possible. "I know it's sounds strange, but I really like playground duty. It gives me a chance to see the children in a different light, you understand?"

"You're better than me. I find the noise deafening."

It was hard to disagree. Jules didn't really like her playground duty at all. Trying to stop children from hanging upside down on the monkey bars, ensuring the quiet ones had friends to play with, and all while trying to break up fights about whose turn it was to swing the skipping rope was enough to leave her needing a nap in the middle of the day. Playground duty was definitely not her favourite, but it was far better than the alternative.

"Don't worry, it's just this one week."

The statement came with only the slightest bit of relief.

"Okay. No problem then. I can do that for you."

Given that he'd got the answer he wanted, Jules expected Gethin to leave. Instead, he moved further into the classroom.

"I also wanted to ask you something else. I was thinking it might be nice to get the staff together regularly, socially. You know, perhaps drinks after school on a Friday. Is that the type of thing you think people would be interested in? I want to put the invite out, but only if I think people are going to come. I don't want to stand there on my own, looking like a lemon."

For a second Jules imagined him standing at a bar, his waistcoat even more noticeable in a social setting. His broad Welsh accent clearly distinctive. Still, it was hard to figure out how to respond. Fridays were sacred to people. Even if people didn't have families, by the end of the working week, everyone was too shattered to want to stay late, particularly if they didn't live in Maldon and needed to travel. They wanted as much of the weekend as they could get.

"Maybe if these get togethers weren't too regular," she said. "Perhaps once a term? Maybe then people would be up for it."

"Is that your way of saying it's a terrible idea?"

She smiled. "No, it's not a terrible idea. It's just weekends are precious to people here."

"That's a shame." He nodded as he paused, though once again, he didn't immediately leave, the way Jules expected, but rather he tilted his head to the side.

"So, does that apply to you, too? Are your Friday nights too precious to go out for a drink?"

Jules considered the comment briefly. Once again, feeling like she was in a catch twenty-two of how to reply. "I mean, if everyone's going, I would definitely try to join you all."

"And what if it wasn't everyone? What if, say, it was just me? Would you be up for it, then?'

CHAPTER 18

Jules's mouth opened and closed as she gaped like a fish. Surely she had misunderstood? Because it sounded like Gethin Jones, her new assistant head, had just asked her out on a date? But he couldn't have, could he? That just wasn't possible. She was still standing there, her heart drumming, unable to figure out what to say next, when he spoke again.

"I cornered you a bit there. I'm sorry." His cheeks had coloured to a deep red and the confidence she had seen in him every time they had spoken dropped as he looked momentarily at his feet. "I need to go get set up for the Key Stage 2 assembly. Thank you again for swapping that duty with me. And maybe you can let me know about the other thing whenever? No rush. I'm sure I'll see you around."

As he closed the door behind him, Jules let out the breath that had been quivering in her lungs.

How? What? Her head was spinning from the shock of the last two minutes. Maybe she misinterpreted his words? But the way he had blushed. No, there was no chance she'd got that wrong. For a moment, she had even forgotten about seeing Flick or Nate at the school gate, as that terror had been totally superseded by her assistant head asking her out.

Before she could recount the conversation fully in her head, a bell buzzed outside and was followed by the laughter of children. So much for thinking she would get some work done before school.

Thankfully, the craziness of the classroom meant that Jules remained somewhat distracted from thinking about Nate. The morning sped by, and there was no denying it was nice to have her break time to herself, rather than being on duty, but while the children sat around on the mat for Friday afternoon show and tell, she found it nearly impossible to stop her mind from wandering.

"That's fantastic Joseph. Really fantastic." She cut through the boy's presentation on his Lego dinosaur, a presentation that had already lasted ten minutes. The child certainly had a skill, describing six Lego blocks in the most extensive way possible.

"Now, who have we got next?"

Immediately, another child was on their feet.

"Dylan, what's that you've got there?" Jules asked, eyeing the small plastic tub the boy held.

Lego figures were one of the most commonly brought in items, but it could've also been something he'd baked, something he'd made, or perhaps a selection of pretty feathers he'd picked up on the roadside. The type of feathers he would try to convince the class came from an eagle, when it was obvious they came from a pigeon.

As he opened it up, it turned out Jules's guess about feathers wasn't that far off.

"It's a snakeskin," Dylan announced, holding up the specimen for all to see.

It really was. There in his hand, the translucent, serpentine skin curved with a mysterious allure.

"Snakes shed their skin between four and twelve times a year," he explained, his voice filled with authority. "It depends on their age and how quickly they are growing. You must be careful holding snakes when they're shedding their skin, because it can make it more difficult for them to see, so they could bite you."

"I didn't know that," Jules admitted, recalling something that had been written on the transfer forms from the class below, detailing this child's extreme love of reptiles.

"So, where did you get the snakeskin from, Dylan?" Jules ventured. "Do you have a pet snake?"

"No, I wish I did. I'm not allowed one until I'm sixteen. My cousin's got one, though. A corn snake, and once it got out, and they couldn't find it for ages, then it turned out that it was in the chimney."

"Really?"

"This isn't a corn snake skin, though. Corn snake skins are much thinner. This is a skin that one of my friends gave me for my birthday. When I grow up, I'm going to have a Burmese python. They're one of the biggest constrictors in the world."

"Well, that sounds fantastic, thank you, Dylan," Jules said, with her voice that meant she was bringing this part of the show and tell to an end. "Now, we're nearly done for the day and I know that you've still got lots more things to show me. Who wants to go next?"

All the remaining hands on the mat fired into the air, but it was Evie to whom Jules's eyes were drawn. She was sitting cross-legged, calm and patient, barely jiggling up and down at all, although it was impossible to see what she had brought. Unlike many of the children, who were holding large objects, from cardboard boxes decorated with scraps of tissue paper to fluffy toy rabbits, Jules couldn't see anything in Evie's hands.

"Evie, do you have something you would like to show to the class?"

The young girl nodded. "Okay, then. Stand up and come to the front."

With her lips pressed tightly closed, Evie stood up, and only then did Jules notice how her hand was clenched tightly. "Why don't you tell everyone what you've brought in to show us?"

Despite her initial keenness, Evie was now looking at her feet. And even when she opened her hand to study the object within, her fingers parted by such a small amount that even with Jules standing right next to her, she couldn't see what was in there.

It wasn't hard to see the nerves bubbling through the young girl, and though it wasn't unusual for children to worry about speaking in a whole-class environment, this timid, reticent Evie was very much at odds with the girl that Jules had seen previously in her classroom.

"Would you like to tell everyone, or do you want to go later?" Jules asked, gently.

Another pause followed as Evie gnawed down on her bottom lip, only to finally open her mouth and palm simultaneously.

"I brought in my dad's wedding ring," she said.

CHAPTER 19

Jules tipped her head to the side, not sure whether she had heard the child properly, although when she asked Evie to repeat herself, she said the exact same thing. Still, Jules wasn't concerned. Children often exaggerated the importance of the items they had brought in. She'd had two children in prior classes who brought in rocks that they swore were from the moon, and one who had tried to convince their classmates that a scrunched-up toilet roll was part of a genuine unicorn horn.

"Well, we would love to see it?" Jules said, expecting Evie to bring out some plastic piece of tat. But there was nothing plastic-looking about the item in Evie's hand.

"It's real gold," she said, pinching the band between her fingers as she showed it to the class.

"How can it be gold? It's white?" One child on the mat responded.

"It's white gold."

"That's not really a thing."

"It is. My mum wears white gold earrings. And my nan

does too." While Joseph came to Evie's defence, others were still ready to dismiss her claim.

"That's just silver. Silver things are silver. That's why they're called silver."

"No, some silver things are gold."

"That doesn't make any sense."

Dissent descended on the mat, as a tight gnawing began in Jules's gut.

"Evie, could I see that for a moment, please?" Jules held out her hand, and the child was quick to respond. Jules stiffened. There was a hallmark imprinted on the inside of the ring and an inscription too. She turned her head away before she gave herself a chance to read it.

"Evie, does your dad know you've brought that in? I think it's probably very precious."

The way the child's eyes shifted to the ground told her everything she needed to know.

"Mummy has one too, but she still wears hers, even though Daddy says he wishes she wouldn't. Daddy doesn't wear his anymore. That was why I took it. It was just in a box in his bedroom. And it doesn't fit me yet, but I know he'll let me have it when it does."

"That might be so, Evie, but I'm not sure you should have taken something so precious without asking. It's very beautiful though, and I feel very lucky that we got to see it. Do you mind if I hold on to it until home time? I think it might be a bit special to have on the carpet."

Evie smiled broadly.

"You can hold my snakeskin too if you want, miss," Dylan piped up.

After taking the ring – and tactfully ignoring the comment about the snakeskin – Jules continued to speak. "Thank you,

Evie. Now, why don't you sit down? We've just got time for two more people to show us what they've brought in today."

Jules barely listened to the last two items in the show and tell. Instead, her mind whirred as she considered what to say come pick-up time.

As the children grabbed their coats and bags, she tried to decide whether it would be best to face Flick or Nate on the matter. Flick had already spoken to her about the situation. It wasn't like Jules was finding out news of their marital problems through Evie, but she could react badly. Nate, on the other hand, would probably be more matter of fact about it. And possibly less harsh on Evie. But that would mean she had to speak to Nate.

One minute before the bell rang, the class was lined up by the door and ready to go.

While some days the parents could be late picking their children up, that was rarely the case on Fridays. Just like the teachers, the parents were ready to get the weekend started. As she opened the door, parents' conversations quickly ended and one by one, she reunited the children with their adults. But she was only looking for one. He was standing on the edge at the playground leaning on the wall by himself. Nate. A mixture of relief and fear flooded through Jules as she tried to keep her smile in place.

"Evie, could you go to your dad and ask him to hang on for five minutes?" she said, when Evie reached the front of the queue. "I need to talk to him when the other students have gone."

Five minutes later it was only Jules, Nate and four parents who were gossiping loudly about how difficult the science homework had been this week left in the playground.

"Evie, hun, why don't you run about for a minute? See how

many laps you can do before Ms Chard has finished speaking to me?"

Evie looked from her father to her teacher.

"You can leave your bag with us, Evie," Jules encouraged.

Without a word, Evie dropped her school bag by the adults' feet and started running.

"Is everything alright?" Nate questioned. "You know, you could have rung me."

"This is about Evie." Jules tried to keep her voice steady. "School. Today, she brought your wedding ring in for show and tell."

Nate frowned. "She did? Where did she even find it? I can't remember where it was."

"That doesn't matter." She took a deep breath in. "She was talking about how you don't wear it anymore and how you told Flick not to wear hers anymore."

"Jeez." Nate rested his hands on his head before turning to watch Evie perform her fourth lap of the playground. "I didn't think she'd even pick up on that. Or know what a wedding ring was. And I've never said anything about Flick not wearing her rings in front of Evie. I try to make everything I say in front of her positive. That day when I saw you in the classroom, that was a shock. I've never spoken so bluntly in front of her before. I promise, I am trying to do the best for her. I really am trying."

"I'm not judging you." A deep ache was throbbing in her chest. She desperately wanted to reach out and take his hand. But she couldn't. This was teacher Jules. Professional Jules. "I'm just telling you what happened in class. So you're aware of how she's feeling. I can't imagine what a difficult time this is for your whole family."

"I find it easier having someone to talk to."

Nate was no longer watching Evie but was looking at Jules

and she knew exactly what he was implying, yet she skimmed the comment like an expert.

"I understand that. That's what I was going to talk to you about. The school has links to several counsellors in the area. Trained professionals that would help her navigate this time."

"That's not what I meant."

"I know. But I think it would be good for her. Good for Evie, and that's what matters."

Nate nodded, his lips pressed tightly together. He was staring straight at her again. His eyes locked on hers. The group of parents were still there chatting. What would they see if they turned around and looked at them, she thought. Just a teacher and a parent having a conversation. That was all that was happening. And yet her pulse was ticking harder and harder.

"You should probably take Evie home. Talk to her about the ring. I put it in the zip pocket on the inside of her bag."

Still, Nate didn't reply, or move, he just stood there. How was it possible for so much to be said when no one was speaking? She didn't want to be so cold and detached, talking to him about this. She wanted to be the one he could unburden to. The one he could escape with. She wanted to say how difficult it was to stand so close to him and not reach out and take his hand. She even wanted to tell him what Fleur had said about fate and the universe acting to bring them together in these moments. But she couldn't say any of that, and when she finally opened her mouth to speak, she was startled by a voice behind her.

"Ms Chard, thank you so much." The voice caused her to jump on the spot. Standing there, his jacket off and waistcoat on full display, was Gethin.

"Your meeting finished already." Jules wondered if she was

imagining the heat behind her cheeks, or whether she was blushing as much as she thought she might be.

"Yes, it was much briefer than I thought it would be, so I came out to give you a hand with the end of the day, but it appears that you've got everything under control."

She glanced over to the gate, where the last straggling parents were finally making their way out of the school.

"Yes, I was just talking to Mr Campbell. There was a slight incident in class today."

"Nothing too serious, I hope?"

"No, it's all sorted." Nate smiled broadly at her, before shifting that same picture-perfect expression to Gethin.

"I don't doubt it for a second," Gethin continued. "I'm sure you know, Mr Campbell, that Ms Chard is one of the most respected teachers in the school. I am positive that whatever the issue is, you are in very safe hands."

"I believe that," Nate commented.

Something had shifted in the air, though Jules had trouble identifying what it was. Maybe Nate was simply trying to avoid showing that anything suspicious had gone on between them.

"I should get going," he said, with a sudden harshness. "Evie, honey, come on, we need to go. We don't want to take up any more of Ms Chard's time."

Turning on the spot, he marched across the playground without so much as a *have a nice weekend.* Jules watched the pair of them go.

"Everything okay there?" Gethin's voice caused Jules to jump for a second time. "It sounded as though he was getting a little combative."

"Na— Mr Campbell? No, no. Everything's fine. There are a couple of family issues that the daughter's picked up on. But other than that, it's fine. Mr Campbell's completely fine."

Gethin nodded, though he didn't look like he believed her. "As long as you know that I'm here to support you. If you feel you ever need a member of management, let me know."

"Thank you. But honestly, that won't be necessary."

Gethin followed with a quick inhale, almost nervous in action, as he glanced down and looked at his watch.

"I realise I said that I would give you time to think about it, but I seem to have got all my jobs done much earlier than planned today. So I was wondering if you'd thought any more about that offer I made to take you out for a drink? Or perhaps a very early dinner? I know you've lived in Maldon forever, so I'm happy to defer to you for choosing a place."

"Oh, I—"

"Sorry, I forgot Evie's bag."

The voice was like a hammer to her chest, strong enough to knock the wind from her lungs. As Gethin too, fell suddenly silent.

Jules's throat had dried. Her palms were sweating. The last thing she wanted was for Nate to have heard Gethin asking her out, yet, as she turned and saw the look in his eyes, she knew without a doubt he'd caught it all.

"Have a good weekend," he said, then turned and left.

CHAPTER 20

Never could Jules remember wanting to bolt out of the school gates so quickly, half to get away from Gethin, half to go after Nate. But she couldn't. Instead, she just stood there, with her cheeks turning redder and redder.

"Tonight's not a great night for me, I'm afraid," she said as diplomatically as she could to Gethin. "I better run. My son…"

"Of course. I don't want to keep you. Have a great weekend."

Jules headed straight to her classroom, where she wrote an SOS message to the book club girls. Before she had hit send, she received a text from Austin, saying he was going to James's for dinner. Which meant Jules had plenty of time for a drink.

By five o'clock, the girls were gathered at hers.

"So the teacher? He's good-looking, right?" Gemma asked, almost overfilling Jules's glass as she topped it up. "And you said he's nice, too."

"But he's not just a teacher, he's the assistant head, and he's only been there a couple of weeks. And I'm not in a space where I can even think about that now. Not with Nate still on my mind."

"Poor Nate, I feel sorry for him." Fleur was on the soft drinks. "He sounds like a lovely guy, and divorce is so tough. I know, I've been there."

Jules sipped on her drink. No matter how much she tried, she hadn't been able to erase the image of Nate's eyes from her memory. That hurt with which he viewed her, like she had somehow betrayed him. More than once she had considered texting to tell him she had turned Gethin down, but what would that achieve? Then he'd think she was holding on until he and she could be together, and that was never going to happen.

"What are you going to do about the yacht club tomorrow?" Gemma asked, tucking her feet underneath her on the sofa. "He's going to be at the sailing club again, I assume?"

"I've already asked Austin's friend's dad if he can take him. I said that we could do lift shares, and next week I can't stay anyway as we have to do set painting for the school show, so my drop-off and pick-ups will have to be super speedy."

"You know, you might be worrying about nothing." Maria was one of the least vocal in the book club, but like many people who didn't speak that often, what she did say was usually worth listening to. "He might not even be there by then. You said it's his friend who is running it. Besides, if he is, then maybe it will give you a chance to clear the air. Work out how you move forward without running and hiding or kissing whenever you see him."

"There is no moving forward, not with Nate at least," Jules said. That was the truth.

"So maybe going on a date with Gethin is the right thing to do, after all?" Sophie suggested.

With another sip of her drink, Jules thought about the

assistant head. The ridiculous thing was, had he asked her out like that previously, when Nate wasn't on the scene, she might have said yes. Though the fact they worked together still made things tricky.

"Maybe," she said, still not sure if she meant it. "I'll think about it."

"Don't do that."

"Do what?" Jules wasn't even sure what Gemma was referring to.

"You're wallowing. I can see that you're wallowing. This Gethin could be the most perfect man in all of history, and you're going to ignore it because you're still hung up on Nate, who you barely even know."

Gemma was decidedly more on the nail than Jules would've liked.

"And why are we drinking at your house? Didn't you just say Austin messaged to say he is staying over? We should go out."

"Going out means spending money, which I don't have any spare of," Jules replied without missing a beat.

"Then I'll pay," Fleur piped up. "I got another bonus at work this month. It's the third one I've got, so it's a bit embarrassing. But it means that drinks are on me."

Jules could already tell that there was no getting around this. All the girls were looking at her. And it had been a long time since she had been out with Gemma, who was normally as bogged down with work as she was.

With just a hint of resentment, she let out a long sigh. "Okay, can we just go somewhere quiet, please?'

CHAPTER 21

As they walked up the high street and passed the White Horse, Jules couldn't help but glance through the window, wondering if Nate was in there. Hurriedly, she shook the thought from her head. What did it even matter if he was there? She couldn't speak to him. Not even to apologise about what happened with Gethin. But that was okay. That was what they needed. Space to forget about one another.

"Where are we going? I don't think there are any pubs this way," Maria said, as they reached the top of town and kept ongoing round the bend in the road. There was a Brazilian tapas place opposite, where they'd been for Fleur's fortieth birthday. They did great cocktails and fabulous food and the owner was the sweetest woman, but on a Friday night it was likely to be busy and a long way from the quiet night that she wanted.

"It's just up here," Gemma said, stopping on the pavement and pointing to a small shopfront.

This area of town leaned towards boutiques. Small craft

shops, with the occasional estate agent and butcher interspersed. She certainly had never seen a bar there.

"It's a microbrewery," Gemma announced.

"A microbrewery?" Jules questioned.

"They do wine too. Come on, let's see if they've got room for us."

While the pace was charming, room was lacking and the prefix of micro seemed to apply on more than one level. As they walked in, they were confronted by low ceilings and several tall tables, all of which were currently full. At the far end was possibly the smallest bar Fleur had ever seen, with several taps attached to the back wall, connected to what she could only assume were homebrewed ales.

"It doesn't look like there's room for us here."

"Don't worry, there's an upstairs," Gemma told them. "Why don't you go get us a seat, and I'll order us a couple of bottles of wine."

"One bottle of wine will be plenty. There are only five of us."

"We'll start with one," Fleur said in a manner that implied there would definitely be more to come.

Upstairs, the space was even smaller, but it had a lovely cosy feel about it. One large dining table was surrounded by seven or eight chairs, while on the other side of the space, two long sofas sat on either side of a dark wooden coffee table.

"I say we go for the sofas," Gemma suggested.

Even though it definitely wasn't a book meeting, it didn't take long before talk turned to that fortnight's read.

So far, Jules hadn't opened the book.

As much as it pained her, Jules struggled to find time to read on weekdays, always feeling like she should focus on schoolwork, rather than indulging in reading a book. Instead, she tended to binge read at the weekend. The perfect day would involve waking up and reading in bed, then not stopping until her stomach rumbled, telling her it was time to move, only for her to start reading again when she had eaten. That was why she loved the summer holidays so much. Those were the days when she could enjoy her books with reckless abandon, not having to worry about the fact that she had started a new chapter just before midnight and would probably keep going for at least another hour. She didn't have much self-control when it came to reading, so this method worked best for her. Now, though, the holidays were an incredibly long way away.

"I can't believe that it's non-fiction," Fleur said as she topped up all their drinks. "The way that first page read. My arms were covered in goosebumps. Can you imagine being that close to death so many times in your life?"

"It was so different from that other book she wrote," Maria joined in. "The one about Shakespeare's son? Have you read that?"

"Not yet, but I'm going to put it on my TBR list. What about you, Jules? Have you read anything else by her?"

Jules looked guiltily across at the group, trying to remember exactly who it was they were talking about again. "I'm sorry. I was just thinking about other things."

"Other things, or other people?"

She picked up her glass and swirled the remaining wine around, losing her gaze in the whirlpools. "Both, neither. Just wondering why it feels like I never get my life together. You know, sometimes I really think everything's about to fall into place, but another hurdle always appears in front of me."

She realised she sounded melancholy, and that last thing she wanted was to bring her friends down, but it was hard.

"First thing," Maria said, reaching her hand across and taking Jules's. "Is to stop being so damn hard on yourself. You have your life together. At least, a lot more together than most people I know. You have a great job, you're a phenomenal mum and you have a group of incredible friends."

As the cheers went up from the table, it was hard for Jules not to smile. The line about the friends at least was true.

"Besides, there are no hurdles tonight," Gemma said as she lifted her glass and clinked it against Jules's. "Just wine waiting to be drunk. And that bottle is nearly empty."

Jules glanced across the table to see, to her surprise, that Gemma was right. One bottle of wine really hadn't lasted long.

"I'll get this one," Jules said, rising to her feet.

"No," Fleur was also straight to standing. "I said I was buying these."

"Really, I don't mind."

"No, no, I'm paying. We agreed. Here, take my card," Fleur insisted, thrusting the card into Jules's hands. "Don't try not paying with it. I'll know when it pings."

Jules forced herself to smile as she took the card and headed down the stairs.

The landlord, who Gemma had said was called Ed, was currently talking to two patrons. When he saw Jules standing there, he turned to her. "What can I get you, love?"

"Another bottle of white please," Jules said as the door jangled behind her.

"Same as before?"

"Yes, thank you."

As Ed retrieved the bottle of wine, Jules debated which card to use. She hated being the friend who couldn't pay their way. Who always worried about how much the extra cocktail was going to cost at dinner, or whether she could afford to take a taxi out somewhere different. But for a brief second, she contemplated using her own card, only to change her mind. Fleur had insisted that she paid. If Jules didn't let her, that would probably mean ordering another bottle of wine, which would mean her hangover the following morning would make it impossible to do anything at all. So, feeling far more guilt than she would've liked, she tapped Fleur's card against the machine, and turned around.

"Miss Chard?"

Given how small the space in the microbrewery was, everybody in the room was fairly close to one another, but at that moment, Jules was standing less than six inches from the woman in front of her. Bumping into a parent in any social situation was less than ideal. She had once bumped into a student while she was underwear shopping in Chelmsford, and another when she had been looking at the reduced food at the supermarket. She had found both of those occasions rather distressing. But it wasn't any parent that she was standing in front of now. No, now she was facing the one she wanted to see less than any other in the entire school.

It was Flick.

CHAPTER 22

Jules didn't know where to look. She could feel the wine bottle trembling in her grasp, her pulse hammering against her eardrums as her breath quickened.

"Miss— Mrs Campbell," she said, her voice cracking. "This is a surprise."

"Miss Chard. Jules. It is Jules, isn't it?"

"Yes. Yes it is." Jules's voice continued to struggle. If she had thought Flick was stunning at school, it was nothing compared to how she looked out, with her hair perfectly styled into loose curls and the meticulous flick of her black eyeliner. Not to mention her flawlessly applied lipstick, which barely creased as she smiled.

"This is a coincidence. I'm rather pleased I've run into you."

In such a confined space, it wasn't surprising that the room was warm, only it hadn't been warm before now, and the temperature was rising with remarkable rapidity. Jules prayed she didn't start sweating. That would just be the pinnacle of her humiliation.

"You are?" Jules said in response to Flick's comment.

It was bad enough having conversations with parents outside of school, but conversations after wine were something entirely different. They may have only had one while out, but the girls had got through another two bottles at her house before they'd left. The last thing Jules wanted was the alcohol to loosen her tongue so much that she said something she'd really regret. She glanced at the bottle in her hand, raising it slightly, hoping Flick might get the hint.

"Are you out with friends or a boyfriend?" Flick said.

"Just friends."

"That must be nice. Lovely."

The stagnation in the conversation was tangible, and Jules was desperate to move. The staircase was only a couple of feet away from her. Unfortunately, Flick was entirely blocking the route. Either Jules had to barge past, wait for Flick to move, or ask politely. The last option seemed like the best.

"We're actually sitting upstairs," she gestured, hoping that would be enough for Flick to move. And yet, still, she remained where she was.

"I was wondering if I could have a quick word with you. I know this is completely unprofessional, but I need to apologise about what I said when we had our meeting the other day."

Jules didn't want to do this. She didn't want to have any conversation with this woman at all, but certainly not on a night out where she was meant to be getting Nate out of her head. Bumping into his not-yet-ex-wife was not helping that in the slightest.

"Really, it's not a problem. It's fine." Jules smiled, yet the act was not reciprocated.

"It wasn't fine. It wasn't okay at all. I just wondered… I

know this is awful of me to ask, but if I could just explain. Just for one minute. I'll happily buy you another drink."

Jules's gaze switched between the staircase and Flick. Not a single part of her wanted to have this conversation, but she could see that Flick wasn't going to let it go. Maybe if she just said her piece, then Jules would be able to go up and enjoy the rest of her night.

"Really, I can't be very long. My friends are waiting for their drinks."

"Thank you," Flick said, visibly relieved, turning to Ed. "I'll take a glass of whatever she's having too, please. Actually, make it a bottle. Would you be okay to bring it over to us?"

"No problem," Ed agreed, and handed over the card machine, which Flick tapped without a second glance.

By some unfortunate stroke of luck, a couple were leaving a table in the corner, and without missing a beat, Flick swept in and grabbed it. "I wasn't really expecting to see anyone tonight. I just popped out for a quick drink. I must look horrendous."

Jules suspected it was one of those things that people who always looked obscenely perfect said. Of course, she didn't look horrendous. She had flawless skin, perfectly proportioned features, and straight teeth that looked like they belonged on an American reality TV show rather than on an actual person in real life.

"What is it you wanted to talk to me about?" Jules said as politely as she could, wanting to hurry the conversation along.

"I'm sorry. What I asked you to do the other day was completely unprofessional. And I want you to know that I didn't go to reception and ask to remove Nate from the contact list. It's just that... obviously you know we're having our difficulties..."

"You really don't need to explain any of this to me," Jules said desperately, wishing she would stop.

"I know. I know I don't, but I want to. You know that Nate and I are going through a rough patch. To be honest, I thought it was the end for us. I was certain it was. I think I imagined to myself that moving here might be a fresh start, there are only so many chances that you can give one person after all. We got together very young. We met doing Model United Nations debates when we were at secondary school. Can you believe that?"

"Wow," Jules said. Nate hadn't been lying then when he said that he and Flick had been together for a long time. "We were probably too young to get as serious as we did. The thing is, he used to be so much fun. He had this smile. It would light up an entire room."

"I know... I mean, I can imagine." Jules tried to cover her tracks, feeling her cheeks burn.

"It's been a long time since I've seen that smile, though."

"One bottle of white wine," Ed said, placing it in a cooler on the table in front of them. "Two glasses?" he asked, placing them down on the table in front of them.

"Thank you," Flick said, then turned back to Jules. "I hadn't seen that smile for so long I'd almost forgotten it existed. But when I came back to Maldon, that first weekend, it was there again. I don't know whether it was the sea or the thought of a fresh start, but something in him changed. That light-hearted, fun nature of the man I love had returned. And I thought maybe it was because he was thinking it could be a new chance for us, too. I didn't treat him very well." Flick said, causing Jules to shake her head rapidly.

"You really don't have to tell me any of this," Jules interjected. "I'm not sure you should."

"No, I've owned up to my mistakes now. And I've made

quite a few of them. I didn't treat him the way I should have, and it was my fault he changed. But I thought I'd got him back. Honestly, that old Nate, he was back with me. It wasn't my imagination. He was there until he walked into school."

Jules's stomach plummeted. Was this it? Was this when Flick confronted her? For a split second she was certain it was, but when she looked up, Flick had this far off look about her. Certainly not the look of someone about to start raging at a woman for ruining her marriage. With that same wistfulness to her tone, she carried on talking.

"He walked into your classroom and it was like all this pressure had returned to him. Honestly, him and Evie had been laughing before, but you wouldn't have believed it, would you? And the thing is, I thought it would be helpful for us to act together as a family. I don't know what changed there, but after we visited the school something shifted. He was tense again. And I thought that maybe if I could just relieve him of a little bit of responsibility, that would help. Does that make sense? It probably sounds horrendously manipulative to you, doesn't it? I think it probably is horrendously manipulative, but I just want you to believe that I wasn't doing it because I'm a bad person. I really wasn't. I was doing it because I love my husband."

Jules could hear the sincerity in her voice, and it felt like a knife between her ribs. If she hadn't felt guilty before, she sure as hell did now. Her throat had constricted so much it was practically closed. With a great effort, she coughed out a response.

"I understand, I really do."

"I just don't want you to think I'm a bad person, that's all."

How did she respond to that? Could Jules tell her she knew what it was like to make mistakes? After all, she had kissed a married man the day after meeting his wife. Sure, Flick might have done some bad things during her relationship with Nate, but Jules was far from blameless.

"I don't think you're a bad person," Jules said when she had finally regained her voice. "I don't think a bad person could raise a daughter as wonderfully polite, generous and kind as Evie is." A bright smile shone from Flick, making her face even more radiant than before.

"You don't know how much it means to me to hear you say that. It really does."

"It's true. She's a gem. And I'm sure that whatever happens between you and Mr Campbell will be the best in the long run."

"Thank you. It means such a lot to hear you say that." Flick reached across and took Jules's hand, leaving Jules to wish the ground would open and swallow her whole. Then, without warning, she stood up and pushed the stool away from the table. "I should get going."

"What about the rest of your wine?" Jules gestured to the full bottle in front of her. Flick hadn't even poured a single glass.

"I don't feel the need to drink quite as much as I did," Flick smiled. "Take it upstairs for the rest of your friends and offer them my sincere apologies for keeping you for so long."

With that, she turned and left, leaving Jules stunned as the doorbell jangled in the air.

CHAPTER 23

Jules traipsed back upstairs with the two bottles of wine, placed one in front of Fleur, along with her card, then took the other and filled her glass to the very top. Only when she had polished off half of it, with all her friends staring at her in mild disbelief, did she pick up the bottle and explain.

"It was from Flick. Nate's wife," Jules said, then promptly polished off the rest of her glass while the rest of them bombarded her with questions.

The next morning, Jules's head hurt. A lot. Every year, hangovers got worse and worse, but she couldn't remember feeling this bad for a long time. A feeling that was made all the worse by the fact she could only remember snippets of the night.

Did we do karaoke? she wrote on the group chat, only for her phone to go wild with a series of photos of her with a microphone. In one of them, she was kneeling on the ground, head back with the mic above her like she was Freddie Mercury at Wembley. It would have been humiliating in any situation, but Jules couldn't sing. Unlike Maria – who could have gone professional – she could barely pitch a note, let alone hold a tune. Thankfully, no one had any videos. At least, that was what they told her.

As Austin was going straight to sailing from James's, Jules should have had the entire morning to be productive, or perhaps even spend time on herself, browsing the charity shops or antique fairs, or maybe going for a walk. Instead, she set herself up in front of the television with painkillers and an enormous glass of water, hoping to feel half human by the time her son arrived home.

Thankfully, the rest of the weekend was uneventful. Having missed out on Friday night films, Austin was keen to curl up with her and watch something that evening, and she even managed to drag herself out of the house and down to the Co-op to grab a couple of pizzas. And while she wasn't feeling entirely fresh when Monday morning rolled around, she had at least planned all her lessons and was ready to work. Which was good, because this next week was going to be a long one; preparation for the school play had begun.

The first school she had worked at hadn't bothered about plays and shows. They had performed a nativity variation each year – "Dennis the Donkey" or "The Angel Who Lost Her Wings" – but it was more out of obligation and tradition than any desire to perform. In such situations, the events took place on a makeshift stage, in front of the normal white background of the school hall.

But St Catherine's was different. St Catherine's prided itself on its performing arts. The hall had a permanent stage, with proper curtains that could be opened and closed during set changes. Each performance was planned down to the minutest of details.

It would be easy to say the extravagant displays were for

the parents' benefit, rather than the children, and that was certainly what Jules had believed the first time she was told she had to give up one of her Saturdays, right at the beginning of the school year, to paint an eight-foot rainbow backdrop. But when the children came in the following Monday morning, and saw the stage transformed, it had all been worth it. Now, she never doubted the importance of doing that job.

It helped that every member of staff joined in with painting. While the day was overseen by Philippa Keegan – the art teacher – the head, Dawn, would be there, as would Gethin, Frances and every classroom teacher. Even Amanda from reception would normally drop in for half an hour to bring them all cups of coffee and make sure it was going okay. Parents also signed up to help, although there was a strict no children rule. After all, they didn't want anything to ruin the magic.

Most schools would never have considered putting on a play so early in the first term, but according to Dawn, it was much better to get these things done at the start of the year when everyone was refreshed, rather than later in the term when the children were tired, and the teachers were juggling assessments and reports and parents' evenings. Besides, it set a precedent for how the school year would go. It was hard to disagree with that logic. So, following the creation of the set, there would be an intense four weeks, in which parts would be allocated, costumes sewn, songs practised and lines learned, all between the normal schedule of maths, English, science and humanities.

"Remember, your parents will need to get tickets from reception," Jules said to her class that Friday afternoon. The older children, who had been through it before, were all buzzing with excitement, which had filtered down to the younger years. All of whom were trying to guess what play they were doing. "I've sent emails out to all of them and put messages in your planner, too."

"Miss Chard, my mum and dad are coming to help you paint tomorrow," Freddie said, bouncing on the mat as he spoke.

"And mine are." Another hand shot in the air.

"My gran is coming because my parents have to look after my baby sister."

Announcements of whose parents were coming to help came from every angle in the classroom, and Jules couldn't help but feel a bit of excitement.

"What about you, Evie?" she asked, hoping for a certain answer. "Are either of your parents coming to help paint?"

Please say no, please say no, please say no. The words echoed around in Jules's head. She wasn't sure she could cope otherwise.

"I don't think so, no," Evie said. "My dad has to work on Saturdays and I think my mum and I are going to see my nanny and grandad."

"Well, I'm sure you'll have an amazing time visiting them," Jules said, doing her best to sound encouraging, though Evie's glumness muted the excitement she felt, knowing she wouldn't bump into Nate or Flick again at the weekend. "You must let us know all about it when you get back. You'll have to tell them all about how well you've settled in here, won't you? Now, time for you all to pack away."

On Saturday, Jules dropped Austin and James at the yacht club, with enough money for them to get the bus home. There was no doubt she was nervous about him travelling on public transport on his own, but, as she continued to remind herself, he was a secondary school student now and she needed to treat him that way. After all, James had been getting the bus all the way to Chelmsford since the start of the summer.

Despite her nerves, and the fact that she was going into school on a weekend, Jules walked in through the school gate dressed in a pair of old dungarees and well-worn trainers and with a slight jaunt in her step. After all, she was painting. Painting made everyone happy. And it would be nice to spend some time with Frances, too.

"Juliana, fantastic. I was hoping you'd be here." The art teacher, Philippa, was the only person who insisted on calling every member of staff by their full name. Jules found it mildly annoying, but not nearly as frustrating as some of the other teachers. Bob, for example, did not respond well to Robert. "We've had lots more volunteers than we thought we would. I was wondering if you wouldn't mind helping create the papier mâché props? I've just sent one parent into my room to get the glue and paper. They looked a bit baffled, if I'm honest. Perhaps you could help them?"

"Of course, no problem."

The school may have been small, but there was still plenty of room for them all to mill about, and plenty of empty classrooms. As Jules headed towards the art room, she thanked herself for choosing the pair of old dungarees, rather than anything she might be worried about getting glue on. She should have known she would get a messy task.

As she opened the art door, the bemused parent Philippa had mentioned was standing in the middle or the room, turning in a circle looking completely lost. But when his eyes met Jules, he stopped, and a smile spread wide on his face.

"Any chance you know where the glue is?" he said.

CHAPTER 24

Nate was standing in the middle of the room.

"You have to be joking," Jules said.

It wasn't the politest greeting to give a parent of one of their students and had any member of staff been near, she would have undoubtedly received a stern talking to, but Jules wasn't thinking about work or other members of staff. She was thinking solely about Nate, who was standing straight in front of her.

"I wasn't sure you'd be here," he said.

"I have to be here. It's my job. Evie said you were going to be at work. And that she was visiting her grandparents. I thought neither of you could make it."

Nate, having noticed the bottles of PVA glue by the sink, made a beeline for them.

"Flick thought it was important for one of us to show our face at some of these events. She's already got it in her head the other mums don't like her from the WhatsApp group. And it was either this, or I sign up for the zoo trip. I figured two hours on a bus beside me would be worse than spending a day where we can move through the school and you can pretend not to see me."

His voice was cool, controlled, and felt like sharp needles in her heart. If anything, it sounded more like the Nate she had met in the classroom with his wife than the one she had been alone with on a boat, where a simple kiss had caused an explosion of butterflies within her.

"Nate," she started, but faltered. She wasn't sure why she had spoken his name like that. It wasn't like there was anything more she could say to him. Not in school. But his coolness confused her until he spoke again.

"So, you and that other teacher, you seemed to get on well. Weird, because some would say that dating another member of staff would be a hell of a lot less professional than dating a guy who you met randomly at a bar."

Suddenly, it all made sense. Jules stiffened. "Not that it's any of your business, but I am not dating anyone. And if you have a problem with my professionalism, then take it up with the correct channels, though I'd love to hear what you'd say."

His jaw was locked, his eyes blazing. "Jules, I—"

Whatever he was going to say, he didn't get the chance to finish. Before he could, the door swung open, and there stood Philippa, her hair wrapped in a coloured headscarf and glasses dangling down her front.

"Fantastic. You two haven't started yet. We're about to run out of paint for the castle. They've got less than half a tin left. I said I'd send someone to get some. One of you wouldn't mind going, would you?"

"We can both go." The words flew from Nate's lips before Jules had a chance to speak.

"Wonderful." Philippa beamed, seemingly unaware of the horror that had just struck Jules. As quickly as she could, Jules tried to salvage the situation.

"Don't you think one of us should stay and make a start on the papier mâché?"

Philippa crinkled her nose as she looked at the pile of newspaper in the centre of the table.

"I'll be honest, I was in two minds about it, anyway. And if you both go, you'll be able to bring some of the other bits and pieces I need."

"Great," Nate looked at Jules, a grin twitching on his lips. "We'll take my car."

IN THE SCHOOL CAR PARK, Jules stood by the passenger door of Nate's car, though she refused to step inside.

"You have to be joking."

"You don't like Porsches?"

"I wouldn't know. I've never been in one."

This wasn't one of the flashy, people-carrier type Porches that several of the parents dropped their children off at school in. This was vintage. Silver. Beautiful curves that she just wanted to run her hands over. It might have been true that she'd never been in a Porsche before, but Jules didn't need to have, to know that she liked this car.

"Well, there's a first time for everything." Nate slid up beside her and opened the car door, before moving around to the driver's side. "Come on. I promise I won't drive fast," he tried again, but rather than stepping inside, Jules stood there, her eyes flicking back and forth between the classroom and the car.

On the other side of the vehicle, Nate let out a long sigh.

"You know, the only thing suspicious here is you," he said. "We were asked to go to the shop together. You looking all guilty is what will draw attention to us, so will you please get in?"

He was probably right, Jules realised. She hadn't had a choice in this. It was Philippa's doing. For school. With her mind made up, Jules opened the door and dropped into the car, only to find it was substantially lower than she thought. She fell with a loud thud, her legs splaying up.

"Don't worry, you'll get used to it," Nate assured her. A moment later, she closed the car door, sealing the two of them in together.

For a second or two, neither of them spoke, and all Jules could think about was how close together they were. Nate's hand, his knee, his face were all within touching distance. His smell was so familiar and comforting that she wanted to take a deep breath in, just to hold on to it. But instead, she closed her hands over her lap, just to avoid temptation.

"So, you and that other teacher…"

"Nate, please don't do this."

"I'm sorry. I am. I wish I could be rational about this. But I can't. I can't think rationally when it comes to you."

She drew a deep breath in. She felt the same. There was no denying it to herself. But that wasn't something she was going to say to Nate.

"We should get going. Sitting in the car like this is suspicious," she said, still looking away from him.

"Okay, just tell me where to go."

The hardware store was on the outskirts of the town, next to a supermarket where they could pick up the other items Philippa wanted, from cotton buds to plastic cutlery. As they moved through the double doors, Nate glanced over at Jules.

"Have you got the list?"

"Yes, and I'd love to know what exactly she's going to paint with this. It'll be enough to do three whole bedrooms."

Nate peered over her shoulder, so close her skin prickled with goosebumps.

"Do you think she's pinching it from school?" Nate asked. "Maybe she's asked us to get all this extra and she's going to use it to renovate her own house."

"Brown paint?" Jules questioned. "No, I can't imagine Philippa is the type of person who would have brown in any room of her house."

Nate raised his eyebrows conspiratorially. "Maybe she's going for the whole boudoir bedroom look. Velvet cushions. Nude women on the wallpaper."

"Who has nude women on the wallpaper?"

"It's a thing. It was very big in the eighties. I could see your art teacher as that type of person. Maybe she's even got mirrors on the ceiling," Nate continued, a smirk tugging at the corners of his lips.

"You need to stop this now." Jules was having a hard time keeping a straight face.

"You're going to think of that next time you see her."

At that Jules burst into laughter. The full-bellied type that she had done so much that night when she and Nate had first met.

"I love seeing you laugh like that." Nate's words combined with Jules's memory of their first meeting brought an abrupt end to her laughter.

She stepped back from him, but rather than moving away, he just changed his position so that their shoulders were practically touching.

"How about we hold hands?" He spoke in a near whisper. "We can walk around here. Pretend we're just a normal couple buying brown paint for their boudoir bedroom."

Despite all she felt, Jules chuckled, though she caught herself almost instantly.

"You know we can't. There might be children and their parents from my school here. Come on, we don't want to take too long getting the paint."

They didn't speak again, other than to confirm that the colour they'd chosen was the one that Philippa had asked for. When everything was paid for, Nate wheeled the trolley out into the car park only to stop and look at her.

"So, I never got to buy you that dinner I promised. But would you say no to a bacon sandwich? I'm famished, and they smell good."

The bacon sandwiches served outside the hardware store were famous in Maldon. Crispy bacon, cooked to perfection, hot rolls. They were somehow a million times better than any she could make at home. And now that Nate had mentioned them, her stomach was already growling.

"Fine, one bacon sandwich can't hurt," she conceded.

CHAPTER 25

"Oh my god, I'm never eating anywhere else again. That's it. My days of cooking Cordon Bleu food are over."

Nate was leaning against the back of his Porsche, his bacon butty already half devoured. There was no denying they were delicious, loaded with onions and brown sauce. Jules struggled to remember why she didn't eat like this every day, only to recall that even if money hadn't been a consideration, her arteries still would be.

"Do you cook?" Jules asked, intrigued. She was making more of a concerted effort to make her food last, considering it more of a brunch than breakfast. She also had no intention of leaning against Nate's car. Instead, she stood just a few feet away, looking straight at him.

"I'm a brilliant cook," Nate said in answer to her question. "Okay, perhaps brilliant is an exaggeration, but I can make damn good fajitas."

Jules eyed him suspiciously.

"Do you use a packet mix for the sauce?"

"Of course, I do. Doesn't everybody?"

She shook her head. "That technically doesn't count as you making them. It's like making a lasagne if you don't make the white sauce."

Dropping his hand to the side, Nate stood up straight and looked at her with mock disbelief.

"You can't be serious. Now you're going to tell me that gravy granules aren't really making gravy."

"Sometimes I think you say things just to wind me up." Jules laughed, taking another bite of her sandwich.

"Sometimes I say things just because I want to see you smile."

The ease that had floated between the pair came to a sudden end. The problem was, when she was with Nate like this, it was all too difficult to remember why she shouldn't be with him all the time.

"We should go back now," she said, nodding towards the car. As she moved towards the passenger side, Nate opened his mouth as if he was going to say something, but Jules shook her head. She didn't need him to be sweet and funny any longer. If anything, she wished he'd return to the grumpy, moody Nate, just so she could believe that was what he was really like.

Without a word, Nate slipped into the driver's side and closed the door.

"What about now?" He said, a moment later when Jules climbed in.

"What do you mean?"

"What if I hold your hand now? Would that be okay? There's no one to see us in here."

A thousand voices screamed out in Jules's head, all of them telling her to say no. It had been hard enough talking with him. Laughing with him. And the longer they were together, the weaker she felt herself becoming. It was as if he had the ability to erode her resolve. The last thing she needed was to let him touch her.

But as his wide eyes stared straight at her, she felt all her doubts piling up.

"What harm can come from holding hands?" she asked and placed her hand on the gearstick between them.

A second later, Nate's fingers interlocked with hers.

It was like a bolt of lightning had struck through them. A spark of electricity that caused her pulse to soar. She knew Nate felt it, too. Jules snapped her hand back, but it was too late. Every inch of her skin was on fire. How? She was a rational person. She never actually believed the statement of *sparks flying* before. But she did now.

Breathless, she looked at Nate. His eyes were wide as he stared straight at her.

"This was a bad idea," she whispered.

"Really? Because from where I'm sitting, it feels like one of the best ideas I've had in a long time."

Then, before she knew what was happening, she was kissing him again.

This kiss wasn't like the others they'd shared. It was different from that one outside the pub, when they'd only just met each other, and different still to the one on the boat, where, despite how perfect the situation was, sadness had enrobed her, as she assumed it was the last time they would ever be together alone. And yet here they were again, this time kissing with a desperation. An insatiable urge to feel as close to him as possible.

This was definitely the last time, Jules told herself as his hand slipped around her back and he pulled her in closer. An involuntary groan escaped from her lips. This was it. This was, without doubt, the last time they would ever do this, but as that was the case, she was going to make the kiss last. That was what she was thinking when the loud knock rapped on the car window.

Jules jumped away, fear and adrenaline rushing through her as she looked up and saw Frances staring at her through the window.

"Philippa sent me," she said with a smirk. "She wanted to make sure you'd got enough brown paint."

CHAPTER 26

"So?" Frances stared at Jules, and Jules, in turn, sank as low as she could into the car seat. After being caught in the act, Jules hadn't given herself time to think. Instead, she'd jumped out of Nate's sports car, thanked him for all his help carrying the paint, and slammed the door behind her. Now she was sitting in Frances's Land Rover, awaiting an interrogation. "I assume you don't kiss everyone who helps you carry paint like that? Otherwise I'd have volunteered long ago."

Jules wanted to laugh. She did. But instead her throat was swollen closed and tears brimmed in her eyes.

"It's not what you think. Or maybe it is. I met him before. In the summer."

Frances tilted her head to the side. "When you said at the beginning of the year that you didn't think you were single any more…?"

"Nate's who I was talking about. Only I didn't know he was married, or separated, or whatever the hell he is. And I definitely didn't know he had a daughter in my class. And now I have to go back to school and paint trees with him and pretend I didn't just have the best kiss of my life."

"In the back seat of a car, like a schoolchild?" Frances mocked. Jules scowled.

"It wasn't in the back seat."

"Those cars are only a two-seater. Technically, you were in the front and the back."

Her friend was simply trying to make light of the matter, as if it wasn't a big deal, but it was. Jules knew it was.

"Frances, I hate to ask you this but—"

"Pfft—" Frances waved away her comment before Jules had even formed the question. "I'm not going to tell anyone. It's none of their business. Assuming you haven't been up to that type of thing at school."

"No!" Jules was shocked at the very suggestion. "We haven't been up to anything. Honestly, that was only the third time we've kissed. God, I don't want to go back to school. I don't think I can face him again. Honestly, I can't be trusted to be in the same room as him."

She had expected Frances to give her some stern warning. Tell her to steer well clear, which was exactly what she already knew she had to do. But instead, her colleague and friend was looking at her with a deep-rooted sympathy.

"Don't go back into school. Grab your car and head home. I'll tell Philippa that Austin was ill."

Gratitude and relief flooded through Jules.

"Are you sure?"

"Positive. Go on."

Jules reached her arms around her friend and hugged her tightly.

"Thank you."

"I'll expect you to return the favour when you catch me snogging Gwen Stefani in the playground."

"Deal."

Back at home, Jules fixed herself a very strong cup of coffee and sat at the kitchen table. Of all the predicaments, this was one she never saw coming, and she had no way of knowing what to do. All she could do was think about how ridiculously perfect every kiss had been. She was still thinking about the latest one, and the way her heart had been hammering beneath her ribs, when the front door opened.

"Austin?"

"Hey, Mum. I thought you were at school."

"Turns out they had enough people," Jules said. She hated lying, but there were an awful lot of parents there. She doubted she'd even be missed. Without her needing to ask, Austin pulled out the chair next to her.

"Well, today was the best day yet on the boats. I've already spoken to them about the idea of helping on the crews, and I don't think it'll be a problem. In fact, one person said there might even be a job collecting glasses for me and washing up. How cool is that? Of course, I can't work that many hours at my age, but it's still amazing, right? Jobs look great on university applications. Don't they? Mum? Mum?"

"Sorry, love? What was that?" Jules hadn't even realised she'd stopped listening until Austin was saying her name and staring straight at her.

"Is everything alright?" His brow furrowed with concern.

"Sorry, darling, I was away with the fairies. You were saying something about a job. Tell me. That sounds amazing. Although I need to check it's legal first. I think you have to be thirteen to work."

He didn't respond. Instead, his eyes narrowed on her with an increased intensity.

"Are you sure you're all right?" he said.

Austin checking up on Jules was something he did fairly

regularly. It was part and parcel of it just being the two of them. But as much as she tried to shield him from her worries, he could read her mood just as well as she could read his, and it had been a long time since he had looked at her like that, with such deep concern.

"I'm fine," she tried to assure him.

"Is this to do with the guy you and Vicky were talking about? The one you were going to go on a date with?"

"What? Why would you say that?"

Her answer was a deliberate attempt at evading his question, while also wondering what may have given him that idea.

"Well, it's just the first time you've mentioned a guy's name in front of me before, and I'm fairly sure you haven't been on a date with him, unless he's part of your book club gang. And, I don't know, something about you seems different. Like you might *have man worries*."

"*Man worries*!" She couldn't help but chuckle. "Trust me, I do not have *man worries*. Besides, why would I have anything to worry about when the only man in my life is perfect?" She reached out and grabbed Austin by the hand, pulling him towards her, before ruffling his hair. Naturally, he made a show of objecting, but it was half-hearted. He loved the attention, really.

Every year, Jules grew more worried that someday soon the teenage hormones would hit and he genuinely would object to her cuddling him. But as long as they hadn't arrived, she intended to make the most of it. When she finally let him go, she was disappointed to find his serious face hadn't faded completely.

"I just want you to know I don't mind. You can have a boyfriend. Or a girlfriend. Do you know that James's Aunt Fiona just got married to another woman? It's totally fine."

Again Jules laughed, only this time her eyes failed to match the smile.

"That's very sweet of you, darling, but honestly, I'm fine."

Austin nodded, though from his expression it was clear he didn't believe her.

"Just because it didn't work out with that guy, you shouldn't give up. Why don't you try dating apps? There are loads. For older people too."

"I am not that old! I do not want to try dating apps, thank you." Jules shook her head and let out an exasperated sigh. Can we please change the subject?" Her tone had changed, to indicate the topic of conversation was over. As such, Austin pushed back his chair and stood up.

"In that case, I'm gonna go upstairs and finish my homework. We've already been given two debate practice topics to prepare for next week. And the teachers use these presentations to consider the team for America. I don't want to give them any reason not to pick me."

As Austin went upstairs, Jules finally moved herself from the kitchen table to flick on the kettle. What did it say about her life, when her son was telling her to use dating apps? Possibly that she should use dating apps. With a heavy sigh, she was tipping an extra spoonful of sugar into her tea when the front door opened for a second time in ten minutes. Given only two other people had keys to her house, she was in no doubt about who it was.

"Hey, Vick, I'm here. Do you want a drink?"

Knowing that Vicky rarely said no to a cup of tea – especially when it was being made for her – Jules fixed a second mug, then carried it over to the kitchen table while Vicky kicked off her shoes.

"You will not believe the morning I've had," Jules said. She was keen to get the whole thing about Nate and the kiss, not to mention Frances, off her chest.

As she handed Vicky the mug, her lodger took it without a word.

"Honest, of all the crazy things— Vicky? Are you okay? You look… strange?"

There wasn't another word to describe her friend's current disposition. She wasn't pale, although she was struggling to meet Jules's eyes and her bottom lip kept disappearing as she chewed down on it. There wasn't a single time she could remember Vicky not being able to meet her eye, other than one incident when she agreed to look after her mother's dog for the weekend without asking Jules first. Jules hadn't been too keen, after all, they only had a box of a garden, and just enough room for the three of them, but Vicky had promised it was small and exceptionally well-behaved. It turned out to be a greyhound with a thing for stealing shoes and the weekend away was a three-week cruise. Strangely enough, though, Jules actually missed it when it went back. But this didn't look like when Vicky wanted to bring a dog into the house. This looked more serious.

"Vicky?"

With the mug of tea between her hands, Vicky pressed her lips together as her eyes stared into the mug.

"I've got a promotion," she finally looked at Jules. "Better money. No more night shifts. It's a private hospital, and I know I said I'd never leave the NHS, but I feel like I should try it, even if it's just for a couple of years."

"Vicky, that's amazing! Congratulations." Jules opened her arms wide, ready to go in for a hug, but Vicky's body remained closed off and rigid.

"Thank you. There's only one small issue."

"What's that?"

"It's in Glasgow.'

CHAPTER 27

"You're mad, aren't you?"

"I'm not mad."

"It's okay if you're a bit mad. I'd be a bit mad."

Jules's tea was turning cold, but she only took the smallest of sips. It turned out she hadn't needed that extra sugar after all. It was syrupy sweet and grainy on her tongue, and somehow it had an extra bitter undertone. Then again, that could just be the fact that her best friend and lodger was about to leave her.

"I'm just confused. Why didn't you tell me you were applying for jobs?" she said, truthfully.

"You know I was unhappy. That I was never not looking for somewhere to move to."

"I know, but I thought Chelmsford. Maybe Basildon. Somewhere commutable. Not Glasgow."

Vicky rubbed her temples, as if she was having difficulty getting her head around the idea, too.

"I know. I do. It was a spur-of-the-moment thing. Oliver's been worried about his parents for a few months now. He was thinking about making the move up there. Then this ad appeared. Honestly, I didn't bother telling you because I really didn't think it was possible I'd get the job."

Not sure how to reply, Jules took another sip of her drink, only to find it even grainier than before. Oliver. Of course. Deep down, Jules had always known there'd be a chance they wanted to move in together, somewhere down the line. But as Vicky had never even mentioned it – even in passing – she'd assumed they were happy to take things slowly. Obviously, that wasn't the case.

"So, when do you start?"

"Six weeks. It's not long considering I've got to find myself a flat. I've had a look online already. There are a couple of places around the hospital. I guess that's where the staff usually live."

"So you've been looking at places already?"

"Just since the interview. I wanted to be prepared, in case…"

It had been a long time since Jules had experienced a break-up. In the eleven years since Austin had been born, she'd not had one proper relationship. And she could hardly call what happened with Austin's dad a break-up. Disappearing without a word wasn't normally how it happened in real life and thankfully, from the moment Austin arrived, she had been far too busy learning about burping babies and how to sterilise bottles to have time to grieve what she'd lost. And so this was it. This was her first long-term relationship ending. And it hurt. A lot.

"I'll pay you rent for the full two months," Vicky said, breaking the silence. "Hopefully, you won't find it hard to fill the room. I'll put some feelers around at work too. I know there are a couple of new staff starting."

"Thanks."

"It'll be fine, you know. I'm sure you'll work something out."

"Of course."

Jules couldn't remember the conversation ever being so stagnant between the pair of them. Once she got through the shock that Vicky wouldn't be there to pick her up when she was down and laugh with her every time she needed it, the realisation of the money she was about to lose sank in. Jules was only making ends meet, and it wasn't just the rent money Vicky paid, which made a difference. It was all the little things she did, too. Small purchases, like buying bread and milk and a new scrubber for the dishes when the old one had worn out. All those little things probably added up to more than she wanted to admit. Vicky had been the family Jules had needed when her own family had barely spoken to her. With that thought, another clamped her hard in the gut.

"You know Austin's going to be devastated?" she said.

Vicky nodded. Unlike Jules's, her mug of tea was entirely empty.

"I thought I'd take him out to the Indian for dinner and tell him over a crazy amount of curry. Hope it softens the blow."

"Sounds like a good idea."

Another pause infiltrated the conversation. Vicky was the one to break it again.

"I wasn't sure whether I should tell him now, or wait a bit, you know, make a swift sharp exit?"

"That would mean me having to keep it a secret from him," Jules pointed out, with just a hint of terseness to her voice. "I'd rather I didn't have to do that."

"You're right. I didn't think about that."

The dining room had always felt big before. Plenty of room for them all to sit around the table having dinner, but now it felt too close for comfort. As the silence swelled, Vicky seemed to be the only one capable of breaking it.

"Maybe I should see if he wants to go for dinner tonight? Everyone raves about the pizzas at Salt. I've been wanting to try them for ages. Do you want to come too? I've heard they do amazing cocktails, too."

The pizza certainly sounded nice, but after the day she'd had, Jules didn't know how she would cope with it hearing about Vicky's new job or hearing about sailing or the debate team. Besides, cocktails sounded expensive, and if ever there was a time she needed to watch her spending, it was now.

"No, you go. I fancy a night in, anyway."

"Okay, I'll go ring them up. See if they've got space. If not we'll go for a curry." As Vicky stood up, she continued to fix her gaze on Jules. "Sorry, you said something happened today? Was it at the painting? At school.'

"It doesn't matter." After such a blow, Jules didn't have it in her to talk about Nate.

"Are you sure? It wasn't about Nate and Flick, was it?"

"Honestly, I was just being dramatic. Everything's fine."

Vicky nodded, though she didn't move to leave. Instead, her bottom lip disappeared again before she spoke.

"This might sound a bit big-headed of me, but I'm not sure you should be on your own tonight. Not if it's been a stressful day. Maybe you should ring Sophie or one of the book club girls. Someone to keep you entertained. Stop you stewing so much."

Jules nodded. As immature as it was, she didn't feel like taking advice from Vicky at the moment.

"Maybe," she said.

"Okay, well, I better go ring the restaurant."

With that, Vicky turned on her heel, leaving Jules alone.

A moment later, she dropped her head into her hands.

A month ago, Jules's life had been so simple. Austin had still felt like her little baby. She was perfectly happy being single, and she had enough money to get through the month. Now all of that had changed. Bills were still rising and now she had to bring someone new into her home. Either that or she had to put her house up on the market. Vicky's comment ran through her head. It was true, Jules didn't want to be on her own that evening. She didn't want to go for dinner, though. And she didn't want to ring the book club girls. There was only one person she wanted to talk to.

CHAPTER 28

Jules waited until Austin and Vicky were gone before she got changed. If they knew she was going out, they would start asking questions, and she didn't want to answer them.

Even as she left her house and closed the front door, she was almost certain it was a bad idea. She and Nate should not be alone together. The incident in the car should have taught her that much. And yet, there she was, heart aflutter, quickening her pace so she could get there all the faster.

Nate had agreed to meet her at the Blue Boar, which was at the very top of the high street. The hotel had several little bars attached, which meant even on busy nights, it was usually possible to find a quiet corner.

Her plan was to arrive early, case the place out, and if she didn't feel comfortable, then she could leave. But when she got there, she found Nate already sitting at a table in a corner of the bar, a beer and a glass of white wine on the table, waiting for her.

"Hey." One word. That was all he said to her. And it was

enough to make her insides crumble. Still, she tried not to show it as she took her seat.

"I was glad to hear from you," Nate continued. "I'll be honest. I didn't know if I would. After what happened."

The flurry of butterflies reached an entirely new level, and it didn't matter how much she tried to battle them. Every time she looked at Nate, they surged again. Jules picked up her glass of wine, hoping a drink might help the sensation to abate.

"I had a rough afternoon, that's all," she thought, trying to sound cool and aloof. "And I thought, why not make the situation worse?"

"Seeing me is not making any situation worse. You're not doing anything wrong." Nate reached his hand across the table, and as much as Jules wished she had the strength to pull hers away, she didn't. "Do you want to talk about it?"

She shook her head. "There's not much to talk about, really. I'm barely making ends meet, Austin is desperate to go on a school trip to America I can't possibly afford and to make matters worse, my lodger got a new job and is moving to Glasgow in six weeks. And if I don't find someone to take the room, then I don't know how I'm going to make the mortgage payments each month."

Nate's forehead creased.

"Okay, so that's not great. But can't you just get another lodger?"

She knew that was the answer, and as someone on the outside, it probably sounded ridiculously obvious. But Vicky had been in her life for so long. Jules didn't just think of her as a lodger. She was her best friend. That's who she was losing.

"I'll have to. It's just stress I don't need. I knew I could trust Vicky, and with Austin in the house that's the most important thing."

"Obviously, it is. I can see that. Do you have any friends that need a room? Any of your book club group?"

Jules sat back in her chair and crossed her arms.

"I don't remember talking to you about the book club. When did we talk about that?"

"On the night we met, you said you knew Sophie – it is Sophie, right? – through your book club."

Jules's eyes widened in disbelief.

"I can't believe you remember that."

"I remember everything. I remember that the top you were wearing had a slight tear just here." He reached over and rubbed a point just below the collar of her top, causing tingles to spread out through her skin. "And I remember the way you moved the stem of your wineglass between your thumb and forefinger whenever I directed the conversation to you, like you're doing now." True enough, she looked down to see her hand on the stem of the wineglass pinched between her fingers. "Jules, I don't want to make your life any more complicated. That is the last thing I plan on doing. But I don't think I will. I don't have a place to live yet. The flat I was hoping to get fell through."

"You can't be serious?"

"Why not? It would solve both our problems."

Jules laughed. It wasn't a genuine, heartfelt laugh like the ones they had shared earlier in the day. It was a high nasal laugh, shallow and aimed solely at the ridiculousness of the situation.

"Having you living in my house would not solve my problems. Trust me. Besides, I don't think my spare room is quite up to your standards."

Nate straightened his back. "What's that supposed to mean?" Given how obvious she felt the comment was, his reaction surprised Jules. But he wasn't done yet. "You're saying I wouldn't be able to live in a three-bed semi?" he asked, a hint of incredulity clear in his voice.

That was exactly what she meant. The confusion lay in why she felt so guilty having voiced it.

"Yes, I have nice things. I enjoy nice things. I appreciate my car and my boats. But don't think I confuse having nice things with happiness. Flick and I had everything. We had a big house, a home cinema and an indoor swimming pool—"

"You had a swimming pool in your house?" If Jules had ever doubted Nate was out of her league, this made it resoundingly clear. Yet he didn't seem to think so.

"What I'm trying to say is, at the end of the day, none of that matters. I'd rather be on a small two-seater sofa, eating pizza and laughing with you as we watch a film, than swimming laps in my pool alone."

"So, just confirming, you really did have an indoor swimming pool?"

"I think you're getting side-tracked," Nate said. He made a move to take Jules's hand, but this time she wasn't as quick to give it. Still, he carried on. "You reached out to me for a reason. You called because you needed someone and you wanted that person to be me. Just like I want it to be you. You believe me about the separation now, right?"

That wasn't a question that really needed clarifying. Having spoken to Flick so many times, there were no doubt in her mind that the marriage had been on decidedly rocky ground before Jules had even made an appearance.

"Yes, I believe you."

"That's a start. I guess it depends on whether you want to go ahead with whatever is happening between us. I know I do."

His voice raised at the end of the sentence, as if he was asking her a question. And he was. She knew that, but she didn't know how she could respond. She didn't want to say no, that was for sure, but beyond that, she didn't know.

"We can speak to the head together," Nate continued. "If your job is your worry, then being open and honest has to be the best way, surely?"

Jules wished she could agree with him. After all, he made it all sound so simple. But she had worked so hard to establish herself professionally. She couldn't let anything jeopardise that.

"I need to think about it." She picked up her glass and took a long draw. Not speaking helped reduce the risk of saying something stupid. By the time she put it back again, the glass was half empty. "I should probably get going," she said. So far, the night had involved no kissing, and she was desperate to keep it that way.

"We should finish our drinks first," Nate replied. "Why don't we do that, and then I'll walk you home? You never know, seeing the three-bed semi might be exactly the thing I need to dissuade me from living with you." It was a jab, but Jules couldn't help but smile. "By the way, I counted the tins of paint we'd used by the end of the day, and by my calculations, Philippa had at least two left over. Plenty to paint her boudoir."

"Don't," Jules said, as images of the school art teacher in her racy bedroom rose in her mind. "I don't want to think about it." Still, she chuckled. The small laugh was enough for Nate's eyes to light up.

As she finished her drink, it was hard not to consider ordering a second. Somehow, a few minutes of conversation with Nate made it possible to forget about everything else. She hadn't even thought about Vicky since she arrived and would love to have kept it that way. But that wasn't reality.

"Are we having another?" Nate gestured her empty glass, reading her mind.

"We really shouldn't."

"Okay, but can I walk you home? Or at least walk in the same direction as you, purely by coincidence?"

Walking home should have been a big no-no, but, she considered, as long as they kept a fair distance from one another and didn't hold hands, any accidental kissing should be avoided. Besides, they both lived in Maldon. Bumping into people was part and parcel of living in a small town. She plucked her bag from the back of her chair and stood up.

"I guess you walking me home would be nice."

CHAPTER 29

There were several ways to reach Jules's house from the high street. The easiest and most direct route involved heading past the secondary school until you reached the bottom of the hill, then taking a left. However, that night, she had no desire to take the most direct route.

Instead, they meandered down the high street. Jules's eyes drifted up towards the sky. In times like this, with the heat of summer still in the air, everything seemed brighter. The days were growing shorter, but the blue skies held the feeling of endless possibility, and winter felt like a distant memory. It was hard to believe that in just a couple of months she would be bundled up in gloves, hat and scarf, battling the wind to get back home. Perhaps she would take the long route home more often, she considered. Just to make the most of the daylight hours.

The ease with which Nate's stride matched hers was uncanny, and the temptation to take his hand was overwhelming. So, to resist, Jules folded her arms across her chest as they walked. It wasn't the most comfortable position to head down hill in, but – she reasoned – it would be a lot harder to convince someone they had merely bumped into each other while walking in the same direction if their fingers were intertwined. Though that didn't stop Nate from occasionally nudging his shoulder against hers and offering her sly grins.

"You know, I don't even know where you grew up," Jules said, quickening her pace as she passed Salt. She wasn't certain if that was where Vicky and Austin were eating, but the last thing she wanted was to have to explain herself to them when she got home.

"Cornwall. Truro, or thereabouts. Did I not tell you that?"

"No, I don't think you did. Is that where you learned to sail?"

"Yup, on the water there. My parents used to say I could sail before I could walk." His voice was light, wistful even, although the casual ease came to a sudden stop when he spoke again.

"Crap," he muttered under his breath.

"What is it?" Jules uncrossed her arms, reaching out to touch his in a reflex, and yet he drew away from her. Flinched even.

"It's Flick. Across the road." His tone was a quiet hiss. "Don't look, just keep walking."

Jules's pulse skyrocketed, and despite Nate's explicit instructions, she glanced across the road. There was no mistaking her. The way her perfect posture glided across the pavement.

"I thought she was visiting her parents," Jules said, unable to hide the fear in her voice.

"So did I. They must've had an argument. It wouldn't be the first time. Just keep walking. She probably won't even notice us."

Jules's throat was drying at the same time her palms were

growing sweatier and sweatier. Why was it that when she panicked, her body completely failed to regulate any form of moisture? "We shouldn't be walking together. One of us should slow down or speed up. At least if she sees us, we won't be together."

Her mind was racing as she tried to decide which one Nate was doing, if any, when a voice rang out from the other side of the road.

"Nate? Miss Chard?" It was too late.

Jules turned her head, only for her stomach to sink. Flick was staring straight at them.

For a split second, Jules thought it might be okay. That she might offer a quick wave and keep on walking. But without a moment's hesitation, Flick was marching across the road to meet them and Jules was rooted to the spot, unable to move.

"How strange, seeing you two together like this?" Flick's smile was so broad it was making Jules dizzy. "Nate, I was going to call you."

As Flick spoke, Jules noted the change in Nate's expression. The way it hardened. The muscles along his jawline twitched as though he was grinding his teeth together, and though Jules was looking straight at him, he hadn't yet said a single word. In fact, the longer he didn't say a word, the more and more awkward it became. Jules could feel herself itching to speak. She knew she couldn't. She knew she should just leave Nate to respond, but the silence got too much.

"We were just walking in the same direction, that's all. Both heading down the hill. I've been for a drink, on my own." The words spilled from her lips. "I was supposed to be with my friends, book club friends. They're great. Brilliant actually." Jules willed herself to stop babbling as Flick's gaze met hers. Or Nate to tell her to be quiet, but he seemed to have an entirely different concern.

"Where is Evie? Why isn't she with you?"

Flick ran her hands through her hair, but though the act was a casual one, she noticeably avoided Nate's gaze.

"Oh, she wanted to stay up with mum."

Nate didn't seem to think much of this answer. "I thought you both were supposed to be staying there? This is your weekend to have her."

"I know, I know, but please, Nate, you know how my mother drives me insane. She agreed to drive her back tomorrow morning, so I thought that I'd come here, have a little pamper and then maybe you and I could do brunch tomorrow morning, child-free, like in the old days?"

There was a pleading tone to Flick's voice. A desperation almost, and Jules wanted nothing more than for the ground to swallow her whole. She looked at Nate, wondering if perhaps he was going to say something to make the whole *bumping into one another* sound a little more plausible, but he was too busy glowering at Flick, a vein protruding across his forehead.

Fearing the two were about to start arguing, Jules stepped forward and looked straight at Flick. "Well, it's nice to bump into you, Mrs Campbell. You too, Mr Campbell." Flick blinked, as if surprised to see her there, while Nate opened his mouth, ready to speak. But Jules didn't hear what he said. She had already turned around and was sprinting down the hill with no intention of looking back.

CHAPTER 30

Jules was tempted to leave a note stating she had a headache and had headed to bed early so she wouldn't have to face Vicky again and feign happiness for her. But as much as she would have liked to, there were other factors to consider as well. Vicky's departure was going to impact Austin too, and she needed to ensure he was alright with. As it happened, Austin seemed completely fine. If anything, he was excited.

"Guess what, Mum? Vicky said I can stay with her in Glasgow. By myself. Well, without you. She said I can even take the train up and everything." From the way he was jumping around as he spoke, Jules suspected there had been fizzy drinks or sugar involved in their meal out. A far more sedate Vicky followed him into the living room.

"You seem to have forgotten to mention the part where I said your mum had to agree to this." Vicky glanced at Jules apologetically.

"You'll agree, won't you, Mum?" Austin used his most pleading voice. "You always let me stay with Vicky."

"Letting you stay with her at home is a bit different. I'm not sure about you travelling on a train all the way to Glasgow," Jules responded cautiously. She didn't want to dampen his mood, but nor did she want to make promises she wouldn't be able to keep. "Maybe we need to warm up with some smaller journeys first. Get used to trains."

Jules expected Austin to be disappointed by this piece of news, but there didn't seem to be anything capable of dampening his joy.

"That's perfect," he said instead. "Because the debate team's first meeting is in Reading. And I know some of the older kids are going by train instead of on the bus. This is working out perfectly. Wait till I tell James. He'll be so jealous."

With that, he pecked his mother on the cheek, offered Vicky a big hug, and fled the room.

"So it looks like he took the news well?" Jules commented as Austin's footsteps hammered up the staircase.

"I think I distracted him with promises of visits. Sorry. I didn't want to feel like the bad guy to him, too."

She paused, and Jules knew she had to say something. Still, it took her a beat longer than it probably should have done.

"You're not the bad guy," she managed eventually.

"I feel like it. Honestly, I really didn't think I was even going to be considered for the job when I applied. I hope you believe me."

"I do."

Vicky took a seat on the sofa beside Jules, hooking her feet beneath her. A short pause filled the air, and for a split-second Jules considered telling her about her day with Nate, but before she could, Vicky spoke again.

"To tell you the truth, I'm terrified."

"Of what?" Jules turned to face her.

"Of everything. Of moving. Of making friends. Of moving in with Oliver. Of leaving a job where I know exactly what I'm doing and having to start all over again from scratch. And I don't know what I'm going to do without you. Honestly, I don't know how I'm going to cope."

Tears brimmed in Vicky's eyes and with it came the smallest flicker of relief in Jules. At least she knew she wasn't alone in how she felt.

"That makes two of us. I'm have no idea how I'll manage. But you don't need to worry. You're going to be amazing. You always are."

With that, the pair reached in and wrapped their arms around one another. It was the first hug they'd shared since Vicky announced her new job, and Jules realised how much it was needed. She should have done this from the start – hugged her friend and told her how proud she was of her. She would find a way to make the money work. She always had before.

The rest of the weekend flew by. Sunday morning, the three of them took a trip to Hyde Hall, the Royal Horticultural Society gardens on the outskirts of town. It was an incredible set up, with dozens of types of gardens, along with an impressive selection of sculptures and an adventure playground that Austin was probably a little too old for, but had a great time on anyway. On Sunday evening, Jules helped Vicky browse through various flat listings online. Most places wanted immediate move-ins or at least within the next month, which complicated their search.

They were in the midst of examining one listing when Jules's phone pinged beside her. Without missing a beat, she picked it up and smiled at the message on the screen.

"You've been on that a lot this evening," Vicky said. There

was no denying her tone, yet Jules tried her hardest to ignore it.

"Have I? It's just the book club chat."

"Really, because it looked remarkably like the name 'Nate' pinged up on the screen just then. I thought you two had called everything off?"

Jules swallowed. With everything that had happened between them, she'd decided not to fill Vicky in on the previous day's events with Nate. After all, she wouldn't be able to lean on Vicky much longer. Now seemed as good a time as any to break that habit.

"We are. We have… It's just… It's nice to have someone to talk to. That's all."

Vicky frowned. "I don't want you to get hurt by this. I'm worried."

Given how Vicky had previously been optimistic about the blooming relationship, the comment came as a slight disappointment, though Jules quickly brushed it aside.

"Don't worry, I won't let it go that far." She was lying, and she knew it. She had already let it go further than she had meant to. After being caught by Flick, she had vowed – once again – that it would be the end of things. But then Nate had rung her when he'd got home, and she'd answered, just to make sure everything was okay. Twenty-four hours later and they must have exchanged close to fifty messages. After putting her phone back on the side, Jules turned to Vicky and smiled.

"How about this flat? This one looks great," she said.

AS UNUSUAL AS it may have been for some people, Jules was genuinely excited for Monday morning. This was the day the children would first see their painted set, and she loved their reactions. Unusually, however, she was also in the dark as to what it looked like. Wanting to get an early peek at the transformation, she headed straight to the hall. Predictably, Philippa was there, adding the final touches in the form of fairy lights and glitter balls.

"This looks fantastic," Jules commented as she approached the stage.

Philippa threw a quick glance over her shoulder, then returned to her work without saying a word. Given how she normally lapped up compliments, Jules moved closer, assuming she hadn't heard.

"Can I help you put those up?" she asked, reaching for the fairy lights. This time, Philippa turned around and looked at her square on, while pulling the fairy lights out of Jules's reach.

"You know that here at St Catherine's we like to think of ourselves as a family," Philippa said.

The statement, a mantra almost, was repeated at nearly every assembly and staff meeting, although in all her years, Jules had never had it directed towards her so aggressively.

"Yes, of course, I know that. I feel the exact same way," she responded, unsure of what else to say.

"I was wondering if you did. You know, I saw Austin on Saturday night in town. He was walking home from dinner. Such a lovely boy, isn't he? And he seemed to have recovered from his illness ever so quickly. So quickly, he didn't even seem to remember it."

The warmth drained from the room as Jules scrambled for a response.

"Philippa, I—"

She wasn't sure how she was going to continue, but it

didn't matter. Philippa had once again turned her back to Jules and was climbing the stepladder.

'You should probably get to your classroom, Juliana. The bell's about to ring. You don't want to be late, do you?'

CHAPTER 31

Jules felt horrendous. It was bad enough when her mind was consumed by thoughts of Nate, but now she had the added worry of what Philippa must think of her lying. This almost overshadowed the anxiety she was still feeling from the lack of a lodger. Adding to that, she couldn't find the lesson plans she'd made on Friday before she left, and one of her children was sick under the desk. All in all, it wasn't a day she wanted to repeat.

After school there was an extra meeting. She took a place at the back and tried to make herself as invisible as possible.

"You look like a slapped arse," Frances commented as she dropped a cushion onto the bench next to Jules. "You'd have thought all that back-seat snogging would have made you smile a bit."

Jules scowled. Some days Frances's humour was exactly what she needed. Today was not one of those days.

"Okay, wrong time and place," Frances conceded. "Anything I can help with?"

Guilt flurried through her. After all Frances had done,

covering for her and Nate, the last thing Jules wanted to do was take things out on her. She let out a long, heavy sigh. "Sorry, and thank you, but no, I don't think so. I just need to figure out how to get a new lodger who isn't some complete weirdo from the internet, a young student who believes it's perfectly fine to blast music out at 3 a.m. or some thirty-year-old guy who's only just moved out of his parents' home and thinks that I'll be his surrogate mother and do his washing."

"That's a fairly specific list," Frances replied.

"I know. And believe me, there are a lot more on it."

Jules was about to tell Frances about some of the people who'd applied for the room before Vicky, when, at the front of the hall, Gethin cleared his throat and opened a PowerPoint on the screen.

"You know the rumour around the school is that he asked you out for a drink?" Frances whispered, her eyes fixed on the front as if she were actually paying attention.

"What?" Jules's jaw dropped. "How do people know that?"

"So it's true? I guess that as you were snogging Mr C in the back of his car, it's also true that you turned him down?"

A flush of heat flooded Jules's cheeks as she scanned the room, terrified that someone had overheard Frances, although everyone else genuinely appeared to be listening to Gethin, who had now started talking.

"I want to know where you're getting this from. How does anyone know that? Do you think he told someone?"

Frances crinkled her nose.

"Playground gossip. But hey, at least it means you've got options. You know, I find our new assistant head quite tolerable."

"Quite tolerable. Well, that is praise indeed."

Jules was still seething as she racked her brain, trying to

work out who would have known Gethin had asked her out. They must have been overheard, she thought, but by whom?

The presentation had changed again and was now filled with three-letter acronyms. Since becoming a teacher, acronyms made up more of Jules's vocabulary than actual words, and she envied people who didn't have to use them. She took a minute, scanning the slide, wondering how this all linked to the first image Gethin had shown. Perhaps listening would have been helpful.

"So if I can open the question to the room, who would like to speak first? Jules?" Gethin was looking straight at her, eyes wide as he waited. "Why don't you tell us how you use some techniques I mentioned in your classroom?"

It was like being that kid at school all over again, caught for talking. Did he know she wasn't listening? Of course he did. This day was just getting better and better.

As Jules walked through the front door, the only plan was to collapse onto her sofa and not get up for a very long time. She needed at least an hour of silence to get her head straight after the day she'd had, but as Austin's footsteps thundered down the staircase, she knew there was no chance of that happening.

"Mum, guess what? I've got the best news ever. You'll never guess it. Try. Go on."

Jules rolled herself into a seated position before looking her son square on.

"Hello, Mum. How are you? Did you have a nice day today? Yes, thank you, Austin, it's so kind of you to ask."

His face crinkled into a mass of frown lines.

"Hello, Mum, hope you had a good day. I had a great day. Really great. Here, look at this."

As he finished speaking, he held out a crumpled piece of paper, which Jules promptly took and smoothed out, noticing Austin's school crest at the top of the page with another familiar one beside it.

Still, she paid the images no mind as she set about reading. These things were always so wordy. It drove her mad. Half the time, she couldn't understand what she was reading. And for somebody who was in the same profession, that was telling.

"Why don't you explain to me what it says?" she said, struggling to remove all the creases in the paper.

"Just the best news ever. Mrs Falkes announced today that the sailing club has decided to sponsor two people to join the debate team. They'll cover the entire cost of the trip to the States for them. How brilliant is that?"

Frowning, Jules examined the paper in front of her.

That's what the other emblem was, the yacht club. And what Austin was saying seemed to align, even though something didn't quite add up.

"Why would the yacht club sponsor the debate team?"

"I have no idea. Maybe they see it as free advertising or something? But, Mum, this is perfect. They already know me from sailing. I should have a much bigger chance, don't you think? We have to do an interview, and write a letter, but I'm brilliant at writing. I'll get it. I know I will. And then there'll be no reason why I can't go. It's fate, isn't it?"

Jules scanned the paper, then put it down beside her. No, she thought, it wasn't fate, but something, or rather someone, that rhymed with it.

CHAPTER 32

It wasn't the first time that Jules had sent Austin out of the house on some false errand so that she could get some privacy to make a phone call. Normally, it was because she didn't want him to hear her swearing at his grandparents, but this time her expletives were aimed in a different direction.

She rang Nate's number, unsure of whether he would even pick up. After all, it was only five o'clock and he might well have Evie, but when he answered on the first ring, she didn't waste any breath before launching into him.

"What are you doing?" she said.

"Jules? What is it? Is everything okay?" He spoke in a hushed tone, and Jules suspected Evie was nearby. His next words confirmed it. "Just give me a second." She heard his footsteps, and the door open and close on the other end of the line, before he spoke again. "Sorry about that. Is everything okay? You sound upset."

"Upset?" Jules couldn't believe he was so calm, easy. As if he hadn't just gone behind her back. "Yes, you could say I'm upset. Austin has come home from school with a letter saying that the yacht club is offering two full scholarships to the America trip."

A pause followed. "That sounds like a good thing?" Nate said.

"I suppose you don't know anything about it?"

This time, the pause extended into an out-and-out silence until, after a moment, Nate cleared his throat.

"I don't see what the problem is. The business wants to make as many local links as possible. We've already made one with the school and the sailing lessons. All this is doing is strengthening those bonds. It's just an advertising fee, really. If you want to think of it that way."

"And you just randomly happened to pick the debate team to do this *advertising* with?"

As the next pause followed, Jules could almost imagine him biting down on his bottom lip, as he tried to figure out what to say. But there was nothing he could say to wheedle his way out of this.

"Of course I didn't randomly pick the debate team. I was never so naïve as to believe you'd think that. But if I offered to pay it for you, I assumed you would've turned that down immediately."

Jules's jaw was hanging open. The whole thing was ludicrous.

"Of course I would've turned that down immediately. You can't just offer to pay something like that for someone. It's over a thousand pounds."

"That's really not a lot of money to me."

"You're not making things any better for yourself right now, Nate." Jules clenched her fists so tightly together that she dug half-moons into the palms of her hands. All her life, she had prided herself on the fact that she'd lived without handouts. Other than the five thousand pounds her parents had gifted her in order to save up a deposit quicker for a house, she had never borrowed money from anyone. And even that she had paid back within six months by scrimping and saving. Jules didn't do handouts. She didn't need handouts.

"I don't need your money to raise my son." Her tongue hit her teeth as she spat the words down the line to him.

"I never said you did. I was just trying to help. I know that with Vicky leaving, it would have been near impossible to find the money. No matter how much you wanted Austin to go. And I never want you to feel like things are impossible for you. Not while I'm in your life."

That was it. That was the final straw.

"Don't you see? This can't work. It can't. I've been ridiculous thinking that it could. We are from different worlds. You must be able to see that."

"No, I don't. Jules, look, I wasn't going to say this over the phone. I wanted to say it to you in person. But I handed in the divorce papers today. It's really over."

Jules was left breathless, and a twinge of sadness struck behind her sternum for Evie and also for Flick. She didn't know the ins and outs of it, but it was clear from how Flick spoke about Nate that she did still love him. But that relationship ending still wasn't enough to put things right between her and Nate.

Her back molars were grinding together as she figured out what to say next.

"So, that's it. The second your divorce is finalised, you just want to jump into another relationship?"

"No, I want to be in a relationship with you. Nobody else. I'd rather be single forever. It's only you, Jules. From the first time we met, it's been you."

Her heart throbbed as tears pricked her eyes. Nate had

created a scholarship to pay for Austin to go to America. It was without doubt the nicest thing anybody had ever done for her. And his words were probably the nicest anyone had ever spoken to her, either. But they weren't even dating properly, and here he was sweeping in trying to be a knight in shining armour when she didn't need that. She had made her own freaking armour. Forged in the fires of her catastrophic early years, and she wasn't going to take it off for some man who didn't even offer her the courtesy of a discussion about it.

Her thoughts hardened as the anger from earlier returned. She had rung him for a reason. And it hadn't changed.

"I think it's best if we don't contact each other again," she said. "This time, for good.'

CHAPTER 33

It felt like a proper break-up. Given how long they'd known each other and the time they'd spent together, Jules knew how ridiculous that was, but it really felt like a proper break-up this time.

On Tuesday, several of the children asked if she was unwell, and on Thursday, Jules missed her first book club in over a year. The girls would ask her questions, and offer her sympathy, or, worse still, side with Nate, and she couldn't cope with that. Unsurprisingly, Austin also noticed that something was up, but then as she let him get the bus to Heybridge and back for the sailing club, he was quick to stay quiet in case she changed her mind.

It was amazing how long the ache in her chest lasted. She had assumed that perhaps after the weekend it would have lessened, but instead a full two weeks passed and it had only got worse. It was as if his absence was physically gnawing a hole in her chest. The lingering summer sun was replaced with a crisp breeze and while the trees turned from bright green to more muted tones of yellow that damn throbbing remained just as keen.

At school she moved as if she were in a daze, smiling and laughing at the children, the way she always did, while trying to mask the deep ache that was stretching out beneath her ribs. It would fade, she told herself. She just needed to keep busy. So that was what she did. Working, Austin, helping Vicky sort out a new place to live and figuring out which of the pans and mugs in the kitchen belonged to her. There was plenty to keep her busy without the need for a Nate Campbell in her life.

When it was time for the Key Stage 1 show, Jules opted to stay backstage and help organise the children. Ordinarily it wouldn't have been her first pick of a job, but the last thing she needed was to see Flick and Nate out there. No, she wanted to do everything possible to stop her from thinking about how she was in the same building as Nate for the first time in weeks.

"Quiet. Get lined up. Dylan, why are you holding that broomstick? Joseph, where are your shoes?"

She ran back and forth, finding the students' props and costumes, and all while pushing some on stage, and waving to others to come off.

It was a fantastic performance. They had some incredibly talented children in the school and the play was interspersed with performances on piano and drums, along with singing. Thankfully, the child who was meant to play the violin had somehow forgotten his bow and had to skip his piece. Jules had a sneaking suspicion that the parents of said child might have been responsible for the suddenly missing bow. She wouldn't have blamed them.

"Juliana, well done. A really great effort today." Philippa smiled as she patted Jules on the back. Since the incident with

Jules leaving early, the art teacher had barely said two words to her. So Jules took this display of camaraderie to mean they were on track for an amiable working relationship again. "Now, come and have a coffee with the parents out front."

Jules swallowed. She knew it was a possibility that this would happen, but she'd hoped Frances could cover for her. Unfortunately, Frances had called in sick for the last two days. Jules was on her own.

"I was actually going to stay back here," she said. "There are a lot of things to clear up."

"Oh, that can wait. I'll ask for some of the Year 6s to help with the tidying tomorrow. Come on. People have been asking for you."

People. Jules shuddered to think who that might be. Still, she was faced with the impossible decision of dropping straight back down into Philippa's bad books, or risking bumping into Nate. Then again, she considered. What was Nate to her? Nothing, not like the job. The decision was made. Brushing herself down, she headed back out into the hall.

She was less than three steps in when she saw him, standing there, talking to – of all people – Gethin. Her stomach somersaulted several times. It was fine; she was fine. She spoke in her head with the same voice she would use when a child fell over in the playground and needed calming from a graze on the knee. Looking around the room, she spotted a parent she knew well and made a beeline for them, only to get intercepted on route.

"Miss Chard." Flick was standing in front of her. She was a sight, dressed immaculately in hot pink with heels that made Jules dizzy just by looking at them. Trying to steady her breath, she fixed her expression with her most professional smile.

"How did you enjoy the show?" She asked the standard

question that began all these conversations, before adding the personalised second sentence. "Evie was wonderful, wasn't she?"

"Oh, it was remarkable." Flick glanced over to where Evie was holding Nate's hand, and Jules's gaze followed. Lingering for just a fraction of a second on the way Nate's lips were moving. "I have no idea how you teachers put this together in four weeks." Flick drew Jules's attention back.

"Oh, well it was the children, really. It's all their hard work. They're the ones that have to remember all their lines. And the costumes. They're down to you parents. I think we can safely say that all the performances at St Catherine's are very much a team effort."

"Yes, I'm sure you would say that."

Jules paused. There was something about the way Flick's smile stretched across her face that made it feel unnatural. Forced, almost. A quiver of nerves fluttered within her.

"Well, it's lovely seeing you. I hope you don't mind, but I need to say hello to some of the other parents, too. I didn't get a chance before, being backstage and everything." Jules readied herself to move. After all, she couldn't a remember situation where a parent had objected to the comment before, but Flick smacked her lips together loudly before she spoke.

"Actually, can I just have a word with you? I promise, it will only be a minute. Two, tops."

The nerves kicked up another notch in Jules's abdomen. She would have loved to have said no, to have asked her to book an appointment and schedule a proper meeting instead, but that wasn't the kind of teacher she was, even to Flick.

"Of course, if it's just a minute."

Jules gestured to some seats in the corner of the room, away from where the parents and the rest of the teachers were gathered. It was far from private, but there was no chance of them being overheard. Not with all the nattering going on. Jules took a seat and Flick followed, crossing her legs in an infuriatingly elegant manner. She wouldn't have had any problem getting in and out of a sports car, she thought.

With the pair seated together, Jules waited for Flick to start. It didn't take long.

"I wanted you to know that Nathaniel and I have formalised our separation."

"Oh, I'm… I'm sorry." Jules didn't know how else she could reply. Her throat was parched and growing tighter by the second.

"Yes, well, it was his decision, not mine. But I can see it now. There was no way to get back to what we were. It just wasn't possible." Jules nodded, hoping she looked sympathetic, as opposed to the nerve-riddled mess she was. "I'll go through the proper school channels for the paperwork," Flick continued. "Separate meetings for parents' evening, that type of thing. Of course, I hope we'll be able to do things together, but it takes time to grow past these types of event, as I'm sure you can imagine."

Jules's chest was fraught with tension, but the truth was, she couldn't imagine what it would be like to divorce Nate. To be cut from his life after years and years together. The pair of them barely had a fortnight and yet she was still there, nearly a month later, pining over him like she was some love-struck schoolgirl all over again.

Still, she nodded and continued to offer her most empathetic look when Flick stood up and stretched out her hand.

Following suit, Jules did the same, only for Flick to take hold of her hand. But it wasn't in some casual, polite grip. It was a pincer. A vice. Jules gasped, confused at what was happening. Yet in the pit of her stomach, she feared she already knew.

"Now, I only want to tell you this once, but stay away from my husband," Flick hissed.

CHAPTER 34

Jules could barely breathe. Flick had dropped her vice-like grip, but her expression hadn't changed. That same narrow smile. Tight lips. And fury radiating from her.

"I'm sorry... I..." Jules began, but her voice trailed off into nothing.

"What annoys me the most is that I didn't see it," Flick said. "I didn't have a clue. And yet the signs were there, all the time. From that very first meeting, where he announced himself as single to you. Oh, you must have liked that. Permission to pounce, sweep in and steal another woman's husband."

Heat flooded Jules's cheeks, making it harder and harder for her to breathe. But there was no way she could leave. Not like this.

"It wasn't—"

"And I spoke to you. Not just in school, but at the bar, too? You remember? Oh, I bet you do. I bet it was everything you needed to finally sink your claws into him."

"Please, Mrs Campbell— Flick—"

"Don't you dare." Flick's voice was as close to a snarl as Jules had ever heard from a human, and the sound was enough to have her cowering. "I have given up everything for them." She let out a small sad laugh. "Even when I saw you two in town together, it didn't click. It didn't. It wasn't until today. This performance, when Nate was looking around everywhere but on the stage. It was like he didn't even care what his daughter was doing. He was searching for something. Someone. And guess what, the minute you appeared from behind that stage, I saw the exact same expression on you. That was until you spotted him."

All the blood had now drained from Jules's face, leaving her blanched and cold.

"Please, I assure you, whatever you think Nate and I—"

"Nate?" Her laugh was a cackle, which stopped sharply as she leaned forward and hissed into Jules's ear.

"Let me make it clear, Nate is my husband. He and Evie are all I have, and I am not giving them up. Believe me, if it comes to a fight, you will lose."

With that, she turned and left.

Jules didn't want to stay in the hall. What she wanted to do was run away and burst into tears, only she was at school and there were other parents looking at her, wanting a conversation which involved hearing how fabulous their child was. One couple was already looking at her, waving. Jules offered a small wave in return, sniffed back her tears, and joined them.

Several times Nate made a beeline for her and each time Jules slipped out and started a conversation with another parent before he could reach her. Then, when she had spoken to all the other parents in her class, and several others in the older years too, and she was nearly out of options, the head clapped her hands together.

"Thank you all so much for everything." Dawn's voice

resonated perfectly throughout the hall. "I am sure we can all agree that was a fabulous performance. Let's have another round of applause for everyone involved." After a short, but loud bout of clapping, she continued. "If all the grownups could please make your way to the playground, then we'll get your little ones out to you as soon as we can. And if a teacher can find a doorstopper to keep the double doors from closing, that would be great."

Doorstoppers at St Catherine's were like gold dust. Every year, they started with them in every room, with the room number or the teacher's name or both written on them in permanent ink. Yet in a month, they would struggle to find half of what they'd had.

Jules scanned the room in search of an elusive doorstopper, only to spot one under a chair. She waited a second to see if anyone else had spotted it. Then, upon realising they hadn't – or that they had no intention of fetching it if they had – she crossed the room. She was down on the ground, her arm under the chair, when she felt the presence standing over her.

She stood up, tension prickling her skin.

"I saw Flick talking to you. You looked upset. Is everything okay?" Nate whispered.

Jules cast her eyes back to the hall where the parents were milling their way out of the double doors, with no need of a doorstop.

"What are you doing? You shouldn't be talking to me. I don't want to talk to you."

"Jules, what did she say? You know I—"

He looked down to see what she had already spotted, his hand reaching out for her. She shifted back and looked him dead in the eye.

"No," she said.

CHAPTER 35

When Jules got home that night, the first thing she did was hide in her bathroom and cry. This wasn't the stifled type of sob that she'd suffered several times since calling it quits with Nate. It wasn't silent tears like those that fell a bit too freely during a sad or soppy bit in a film. It was a full, belly-hurting weep which had her nose running as she struggled for her breath. And the worst thing was, she didn't even know what was causing the tears. Or rather, what was the main cause? Flick. That was up there. So was Vicky leaving, and so was the fact that she couldn't do everything for Austin that she wanted to do. She felt like a failure as a mum. It was that simple. And it hurt so badly.

The next morning, the pain hadn't lessened.

"I don't think you should go to work, Mum. You look like crap," Austin said over breakfast.

"Just tired, that's all," Jules replied, but Vicky was on her son's side.

"I think it might be more than that. Maybe you're coming down with something."

Jules shook her head to reply that she was fine. Only the action caused a headache to pound behind her temples.

"You're right. I think I might go back to bed and ring in sick," she said.

In the end, Jules took Thursday and Friday off. It was the first time at St Catherine's she had been off because she was ill. And it was safe to say she felt terrible. But guilt could do that, couldn't it? She was tempted to miss Monday too, only Friday was the school trip to Colchester Zoo and there were still things she needed to do for it. So on Monday morning, still pale-faced and weepy, she headed back to work.

Naturally, as she was feeling like rubbish, with her unwashed hair scraped back and not a scrap of makeup on her face, Gethin was the first person she saw. "Glad to see you're feeling better," he said, patting her arm. "But take it easy, okay? Don't push yourself. You look like you could have done with a couple more days off, if I'm honest."

"Oh. Thanks." Jules wasn't quite sure how else to respond to Gethin telling her – in the politest way possible – that she looked like crap. Frances was a lot less subtle.

"It's not contagious, is it?" she said, hovering behind her before she took a seat in the staff meeting. "I don't want to catch something before Friday. You know the zoo trip is my highlight of the term."

"It's definitely not contagious," Jules assured her. Guilt and heartbreak weren't, as far as she knew, possible to catch.

Still, with everyone giving her a wide berth Jules kept her head down and tried to catch up on work from the days she had missed. She'd only just got on top of things when Friday rolled around.

Along with Jules, Esther – the Year 1 teacher – was also going on the trip with her class. As the whole school P.E. teacher, Bob, pretty much went on every trip going, while the other teacher was Frances. Having arranged the trip for years, she had refused to give it up even once she became head and after she'd stepped down from the role. Though, as always, she insisted vocally that each year was going to be her last.

As expected, Jules found her friend ordering around the bus driver.

"Thank god you're here," she said when she saw Jules. She promptly pulled a large plastic folder from her bag on the ground.

"Here are all the class lists for the register, the group lists for the bus and the group lists for the zoo, which are slightly different because of numbers. The groups have animal names, because Amanda thought that would be fun, and the animal names have been assigned to the chaperones on a separate page, because apparently deforestation doesn't matter. Can you make sure the other teachers get a copy of each of page, please?"

"No problem."

"Thank you. I've also printed off a list of parent volunteers. If you can give them a copy of the zoo groups, that would be great."

"Zoo groups only for parents," Jules repeated, assuring Frances she knew what she was doing.

"Wonderful. They're all starting to come now. Why they need to be so early, I have no idea. And why this bus driver thinks I'm okay with a bus without a toilet when I am about to transport a load of six- and seven-year-olds is beyond me, but I know he's going to get on the phone to his boss and change it. Pronto."

Jules backed away to give Frances the space to deal with the bus and tried to recall the things she had told her as she opened the folder and checked through the pages. The children's list made sense. The bus groups were obvious and, best of all, Nate's name was nowhere to be seen, and neither was Flick's. After double checking just in case, she let out a sigh of relief. With that issue sorted, she was free to enjoy the day.

Just like the school performance, Jules loved the zoo trip and not just because of how much fun the children had there. When she had been a child, trips to the zoo were one of her favourite ways to spend a Saturday. She would coo over cute marmosets and look on in awe at the majestic tigers, although her absolute favourite was always the otters. There was something about the way they chatted to each other, dipping and diving or playing with the toys the keepers had placed in their houses that made them so relatable.

Hopefully, the group of children she was with would want to spend a decent amount of time at the otters, too.

It didn't take long before they started arriving in their droves.

"He hasn't been able to sleep all night," Dylan's mum said to her as she dropped him off. "He's so excited about seeing the reptile house. I'm not even sure why. We take him there at least once a month. He's got a pass that means he can go as many times a year as he wants. I'm sure they know him by name."

"I know the reptile keepers by name," Dylan told her. "Jason is the one in charge of the boa constrictors. He puts their food in and he's the only one that can hold Esme. She's the biggest there."

"Is that so?" Jules exchanged a glance with his mother and smiled. "Well, how about when we get to the reptile house, you're the one who shows us around?"

"Can I? I know all the animals there. Unless they got some new ones in the last two weeks. One of the chameleons died, which I was really sad about, but then they said they're getting another and hopefully, it's going to be a mating pair. Did you know that chameleons mate—"

"Okay, Dylan, I think we'd better let Miss Chard get on with sorting everything out. Don't you?" She offered Jules an apologetic smile before she hugged her son goodbye.

All the children had been told to bring packed lunches and bottled water, so there was nothing to worry about on that end. Really, it was just a case of making sure they had all the children, staff and parent volunteers on the bus with their seatbelts on before they left.

"I'm really looking forward to this," one mum said as she climbed on board, the first of Jules's parent helpers.

"I've given Max a travel sickness tablet," a dad who wasn't staying told Jules. "They're meant to last six hours, but to be honest, it's all in his head. I've told him I've given you some extra ones, but I don't want him having them, so can you just give him one of these instead?" The dad handed Jules a pack of fizzy sweets. "He thinks they're travel sickness tablets."

Jules smiled. "I remember those days myself, often."

One by one, the parents and children arrived, some to drop off, some to join them, although when Jules checked her watch at 8:05, she was slightly concerned that she was still missing some students.

"So, who are we still waiting for?" Frances asked, tapping at her watch impatiently.

"So far, we've got three children missing, Oscar, Safiya and Evie," she tried to say the name as neutrally as possible, "and, as for parent volunteers, we're missing one. I thought Joseph's mum was coming with us, but Joseph is on the bus and she's not here. Maybe she's just parking the car or something." No sooner had Jules said the parents' and children's names than three more cars turned into the car park. Two large SUVs, but it was the smaller, sleeker, sportier-looking car that caught her attention.

As Nate climbed out of the car, Jules turned to Frances.

"I'm just going to go on the coach, make sure everybody's getting their seatbelts on, that type of thing," she said. Frances offered her a withering look, though Jules paid it no mind as she hurried aboard.

On the coach, the children were having difficulty staying put, mainly because of their excitement.

"I can't wait to see the goats," one child said.

"Why would you care about goats? You can see goats anywhere. My uncle has got goats."

"I like the goats. They're funny. They make me laugh more than other animals."

"I want to see the great white sharks." Another said. "Do they have great white sharks, Miss Chard?"

Jules, who was glancing out of the window, turned back briefly to the child as she spoke. "I don't think so, no. You normally find sharks at an aquarium, not a zoo."

While the girl's face fell, Jules's attention was fixed back outside where Evie was skipping ahead of Nate, who was currently holding her rucksack slung over his shoulder.

"Okay, seatbelts on everybody, we should be leaving in the next ten minutes."

As much as Jules would have liked to have hidden on the bus and avoid Nate altogether, that would involve questions from Frances she didn't want to deal with. Besides, one of the other children was in her class, and it was only right that she was the one to meet her.

"We've given her money for the gift shop," Safiya's mum said, ushering her child onto the bus, while the last Year 1 child was running towards the other bus.

Then somehow, the only people left outside with her were Frances, Nate and Evie.

"Well, I'm going to check with the office and make sure there's nothing we've forgotten," Frances said, offering Jules a less-than-subtle look as she disappeared.

"I'm going to go and get a seat next to one of my friends," Evie said, bounding up the steps with barely a second glance towards Jules or a goodbye to her father.

"No problem," Nate said, watching Evie, before turning and looking Jules straight in the eye. This was the closest they'd been in weeks and it was turning her to jelly. The sooner she was back on the bus the better.

"I'm sure she'll have a really fantastic day," Jules said, speaking to Nate in her most professional voice. "And pick-up time should be three-thirty as normal. The school office will send a message should we be running late for any reason."

"Oh," Nate said, a deep furrow in his brow, that Jules assumed was too do with the normal pick-up time. "Did nobody mention? There was a change in volunteers. I'm coming with you."

CHAPTER 36

Jules stared at Nate. There was a good chance her mouth was hanging slightly open too, as she could feel the air flowing into her lungs, but it was still a solid minute before she could speak.

"No, you're not down as one of the parent volunteers," she said.

"I know. There was a message that went out on the parents' chat this morning. Joseph's mum has come down with a bug and wasn't able to make it. She didn't want to stress the school by letting them know."

"So you volunteered?"

"It seemed like the only decent thing to do."

His eyes were locked on hers now, utterly unreadable. There was no trace of a smile on his lips, but his eyes were so damn deep she could have fallen straight into them.

"Well, that's very kind of you, Mr Campbell, isn't it?" Frances appeared behind them. "Thank you ever so much for stepping in last minute. If you grab a seat near the front, I'll just check the last few things with Miss Chard here and we'll be on our way."

"Did you know?" Jules hissed at Frances the moment Nate was on the bus.

"Scout's honour I didn't. But I thought you'd be pleased if I'm honest. The last time I saw you two together, you were sucking his face off."

Jules grimaced at the memory.

"Well we've ended things. Again. I can't be with him. I can't."

Frances's smile twisted. "Why? Because you still like him? You do, don't you? This is fun. I've never seen you hung up on a guy before."

Jules offered the deepest scowl she could in response. She was grateful Bob was already on the bus, likely already asleep, but there was still the Year 1 teacher and a couple of parents who could easily eavesdrop. With her jaw still locked, she rubbed her temples. Headaches at the end of school trips, after hours of listening to children jabbering on in the back of the bus, were expected. Headaches before the school trip had even started were less common. But she could already feel the heat budding behind her temples, a pressure building.

"I'm not getting into it now. It's over, and it's for the best."

"Well, if it's as over as you say, then it won't be any problem being on the trip with him, will it?" Frances's smile flickered with pure mischief. "This school trip just became a lot more fun."

JULES TOOK a seat on the front row, on the same side as Nate, hoping this would stop her from inadvertently catching his eye. For a large portion of the journey, The plan worked reasonably well, although it didn't prevent her from having to pace up and down the aisle to check on the children and each time she did that, her gaze wandered, without control, down to look at him. Every time he was staring straight back at her, that same, heart-wrenching look in his eyes.

While Jules did all she could to avoid any sort of conversation with Nate, Frances, on the other hand, chose a seat directly opposite him, and seemed determined to wheedle every last titbit of information from him, all of it loud enough for Jules to hear.

"So, Mr Campbell, what exactly do you do?" Frances started with the normal questions. "I presume you're self-employed if you can take a day off for a trip like this? Or are you a stay-at-home dad? I shouldn't be so quick to judge."

"No, you're right. I run my own business in boating. A bit of everything, brokering, sailing clubs.'

"That sounds very exciting. Jules, didn't your son, Austin, recently take up sailing?"

Jules's teeth ground together as she shot her friend a glowering look across the aisle.

"Yes, he did."

"Actually, I'm involved with that," Nate continued as if Frances hadn't caught them snogging only a couple of weeks beforehand. "I've met Austin a couple of times now. He seems like a great kid."

"He is," Frances replied. "He's wonderful. And so is Evie. Is she your only child?"

"Yes, just the one."

Jules glanced at Bob, who had taken the front-row seat across the aisle from her, and wondered if she could feign sleep too. It was certainly a great way to get out of doing their job properly. In the end, she tuned out the conversation, focusing on a map of the zoo and trying to determine the best route for their group. All she had to do was get through this bus journey. Then she'd have hours to forget about Nate as she enjoyed the zoo. She could get through this. She could absolutely get through this.

By 9:15, despite a handful of traffic jams, they arrived at the Colchester Zoo car park, with the children bouncing in their seats.

Unlike the rest of Essex, known for its flat terrain, Colchester Zoo was built on an old quarry and was comprised of a series of ups and downs, a real workout for the thighs. It was another reason they liked to start the day early. Children's walking paces were slow, and if they didn't start early, they'd end up missing out on things.

"Okay," Jules announced, signalling the children to unbuckle their seat belts as Bob snorted into life. "Stay seated for a minute. We have a few things to go through. You'll be divided into four groups, each with a parent and a teacher." Just as Jules was about to tell the children their groups, Frances rose from her seat.

"I hope you don't mind, Miss Chard, but as the senior teacher on the trip, I'd like to read out the list."

Senior teacher? Jules thought. Frances had never lauded her status as a senior teacher, especially not when it meant doing something. Yet she snatched the paper from Jules's hands.

"Right, Group A is as follows. Listen carefully – you're going to be with me and Mrs Ferguson."

As soon as she heard the group's allocation, Jules knew precisely what game Frances was playing.

"Mrs Vernon? Can I just talk to you a moment?"

Frances pretended not to hear as she read out the second group.

Just as Jules had anticipated, Frances announced the pairings: Esther was with a Year 1 parent, Bob was with a Year 2, which meant there was only one option left for the last group.

"And the final group will be with Miss Chard and Evie's dad, Mr Campbell." Frances threw Jules a triumphant smile. "I hope you all have a wonderful day.'

CHAPTER 37

While Frances was the first off the bus, allocating the children into their groups and checking they'd all remembered to take their packed lunches off the coach. Jules waited until everyone else, including Nate, had disembarked. Afterwards, she did a once up and down the aisle to make sure nothing was forgotten. When she finally stepped off, she was immediately accosted.

"Are we going to the reptile house first?" Dylan stood straight in front of the bus, giving Jules zero room to move. "I know what order I want to tell people about everything. Should I let you know?"

"We're not even in the zoo yet, Dylan." Jules forced herself to smile. "You can let me know when we're with the others. But for now, please can you join your group? I'll be with you in a second." She glanced over to where Nate was fielding questions from every direction and a slight smile rose to her lips, only for her to quash it immediately. It didn't matter how good he looked. Today was about survival, and as little contact with him as possible.

Several of the children were still fixing their bags onto their backs, while others continued to look at her with eager anticipation. Dylan was bouncing on his toes, desperate to go. But Jules still had to give them the lie of the land.

"I need you to remember you are not to leave this group. We are the largest group, with eight of us here. But you were all chosen because you are super responsible." She watched the children's faces beam up at her, clearly excited. "I am going to give you a copy of the map. Now, we are starting at the rhinos—"

"What?" Dylan objected loudly. "I thought we were starting at the reptiles?"

Jules offered him a withering look. As a rule, she tended not to glare at her children – a slightly disappointed face was normally more than enough to make them toe the line – but it was different on a school trip. If she didn't set the expectations at the beginning, she could be looking at chaos.

"Now," she carried on. "If we listen to all my instructions, and we don't have to stop for any reason, we should be able to see all the animals. But to start with, I want you to look at the map, and decide which is the best way to get there. That's how we are going to do it today; I'm going to tell you where we're going, and you're going to plan us the routes. Got it?"

Lots of nodding heads and "Yes, Miss"s followed, and Jules couldn't help but smile.

"Great, now I don't want any arguing or shouting. When you've figured it out, I want one person to raise their hand and tell me. You've got three minutes to work it out while I talk to Mr Campbell."

With the children occupied and huddled around the map, Jules took a step away from the group.

"You're amazing with them," Nate said as she approached. "No wonder Evie loves being in your class so much."

"Thank you." Jules accepted the compliment as detachedly as she could. "It would probably be best if one of us walks in front of the children to lead the way and one walks at back."

"It's eight children, Jules. I'm sure we can walk side by side. I suspect that's what all the other teachers and parents are doing."

Jules drew in a long breath. Of course they were. But if she walked next to Nate, she would talk to him and see him smile and her resolve would weaken.

"Why are you here, Nate? You could have let one of the other parents volunteer."

"Then another parent would get to spend the day with you." He let out a sigh. "I know you've made your thoughts about this clear, but I'm having a hard time letting go. You know as well as I do this doesn't happen that often. Finding someone that makes you laugh and feel the way you make me feel. I'm not willing to give up on it that easily. Besides, your friend obviously doesn't think there's a problem with it, otherwise she wouldn't have put us together. She is the one who caught us, you know..."

Jules shook her head. The last thing she needed was to be reminded of that kiss. Of any of the kisses. Thankfully, before she formed a response, one of the children called out from the group.

"Miss Chard, Dylan's hogging the map! He says the only way to get to the rhinos is to go through the reptile house, and it's not. It's definitely not."

Plastering a smile on her face, Jules offered Nate one more glance as she turned to her class. "Right, let's go get our tickets. And perhaps it's best if I lead the way for this first part."

CHAPTER 38

After fetching the tickets, most of the children wanted a toilet break, followed by a morning snack, after which it was time to get walking. Thankfully, with the rhino signs clearly posted from only a few feet into the zoo, Dylan didn't persuade the others that a walk via the reptile house was the best bet.

Despite Jules's suggestion that she go at the front, she had somehow ended up at the back, next to Nate. She tried her best to ignore him, but it wasn't that easy.

"She signed them," Nate said quietly. "I thought you might want to know. Flick's not contesting anything."

Jules bit down on her tongue. Nate knew nothing about her conversation with Flick at the school performance, but she didn't know if that made her feel better or worse. Perhaps it was a good thing. Perhaps the fact that Flick had said nothing meant she didn't see Jules as a threat after all and wasn't that what she wanted? Yet before she could think how to reply, she was hit by a wall of noise.

"The rhinos are here! We've reached the rhinos!"

"There's a baby!" One child up front yelled.

"There are zebras there too!"

"And giraffes! I can see the giraffes!"

The children that only moments before, had been walking at a quick but measured pace were now running in a flat-out sprint towards one of the viewing platforms.

"Slow down!" Jules called after them, although as she looked to her side, she discovered that Nate had gone too, and was racing away after them. There was no choice now, she knew. She had to run too.

By the time Jules reached the top of the viewing platform, the children and Nate were all standing gaping over at the field where a selection of African animals were grazing.

"Did anybody listen to what I said about not running off?" Her teacher voice cut sharply, and every single child, including Dylan, looked at her with their eyes bulging. Even Nate seemed to pale slightly. "That was absolutely ridiculous, Year 2, and I'm very disappointed in you." Those were the words that struck home the most. Children's gazes dropped. Lower lips protruded. Still with her eyes scanning each and every one of them, Jules continued her reproach. "This is not a safe place to run off. And if that happens again, then we will spend the rest of the day in the picnic area and the only animals you will see are the pigeons. Is that clear?"

"But Miss—" Dylan began, only to cut himself short at the strength of Jules's glower.

"Is that clear?" she repeated.

All the children nodded.

"Fine. Now you can look at the rhinos."

It was a much more subdued group of children that turned their back to Jules and began cooing over the admittedly cute baby rhino. Nate sidled up beside Jules.

"I didn't realise you could be so scary." His lips quirked with a smile, which Jules did not reciprocate.

"I'm mad at you too," she said. "You ran off."

"In my defence, I ran off so I could keep after the children. And they're all fine."

Jules sucked in a reply. She wouldn't be drawn into a conversation with Nate. Not when he would try to sweet talk her. She was holding her own.

"I think I'm going to look at the baby rhino, too," she said, and joined the children.

A moment later, Nate was right beside her and talking away, though this time he was talking to the group.

"Did you know that rhinos' horns are actually made from hair?" he said to them. "And in the wild, to stop poachers, they chop them off."

"Why would they do that?" It was Evie who spoke to her father with a look of pure shock.

"Well, unfortunately, rhinos get hunted for their horns. So people decided it was better to cut their horns off so that the rhinos could stay alive, rather than have people try to poach them."

"Poach them? Isn't that cooking?" It was a small boy, Harri, who asked.

"Well, yes, but no…" Nate started to stutter.

"Do people poach giraffes too?"

"What about the zebras?"

A series of questions followed about what poaching was and wasn't, along with some of the various methods used to protect animals in the wild, and Jules couldn't help but smile as she watched Nate answer them all. It was bizarre, given how much time she had spent with Evie, and the time she had spent with Nate, that she had never really seen the two interact before. But he had such a natural ease around the children, injecting just enough humour into the conversation so that they didn't get upset.

"Okay, we need to get moving again. Who's got the map?" Jules sidled up to Nate, unable to suppress the smile on her face after the discussion had gone on for a solid five minutes. She could have listened to him talk for longer – and she suspected he wouldn't have minded – only there was a lot to get done, and the children always got tired as the day went on. She needed to use the energy they had in the morning to see as much as possible. "Okay, children, who's got the map? We want to go to the hyenas next. I want you to tell me in left and right turns how we're going to get there."

The morning went by in a series of laughter, with only some mild disappointments. The penguins refused to come out of their huts, and the lion was hidden behind various trees and bushes. But the cheetahs had got a deflated football that they were kicking around as if they were house cats, and they reached the small-clawed otters just in time for feeding time. As the children were chatting about which of them could catch an otter the quickest, Jules reined the conversation in.

"Okay, boys and girls, we've got a real treat today. We are going to listen to a talk from a zookeeper, and I think he might even have some animals for us to hold."

"What sort of animals? Big animals?"

"No, probably not. I think it will be insects." Jules did her best to manage their expectations. "And after that, we'll have lunch."

"What about the reptile house?" Dylan piped up, the disappointment clear on his face. "The reptile house was right by the rhinos. We should have gone there first."

"We're going to go back the same way to go to the picnic park for lunch, Dylan. Don't worry, it's all planned. Now, let's get going, because I want to see Mr Campbell hold a tarantula, don't you?'

CHAPTER 39

"You're not really going to make me hold a tarantula, are you?" Nate asked as they made their way towards the education centre. "I know it's not very manly of me, but I really don't like insects."

"You're right, that really isn't manly. Think of this as payback."

"Payback for what?"

"Well, the debate team debacle to start with."

He paused and lowered his gaze to the ground; when he lifted his eyes, his smile had lowered.

"You know I was only trying to help, don't you? I'd never have done it if I'd thought it would come between us. You know that, right? I'd never do anything to drive you away."

Jules scanned the surrounding area, checking that none of her children were eavesdropping, but they were all way ahead of them, and chatting away.

"It was for the best. You and I, whatever we were, was never going to work."

"I think you're wrong." Nate stopped in his tracks,

prompting Jules to do the same. "I think you're wrong and I think you know it, too. You are I were going to work. I would have bet my life on it."

Jules drew her bottom lip in and chewed down on it. How did he do this? How did he have the ability to completely weaken her resolve every time she was near him? This was why she had cut contact. This was why he shouldn't be there.

"Come on, we need to get to the education centre."

THE INTERACTIVE CLASS with the insect expert came with an unexpected highlight.

"Who else would like to hold the stick insect?" the zookeeper running the session asked the group. Most of the children had already had a go, with Dylan desperately after a second turn. Some of them, however, were less keen on holding the long-legged creature.

"I thought it was just spiders you didn't like," Jules said as she watched Nate shrink into himself.

"I think it might be all long-legged invertebrates, actually." Nate was looking decidedly pale as he stared at the zookeeper, who was letting the animal walk his up arm towards his neck. It was something Jules wouldn't have been keen on either, but she was fine with having it on the palm of her hand. Still, she stepped forward.

"I think Mr Campbell would like a go," she said.

Nate shook his head rapidly. "Mr Campbell is absolutely fine, actually."

Jules grinned. Yes, it was the type of payback she needed.

"Evie, what do you think? Should your dad have a go at holding the stick insect?"

At this, Evie bounced on the spot excitedly.

"Yes! Go on, Daddy, you can do it. I did it."

"I'll do it if Miss Chard holds it first," Nate said. A smirk graced his lips, he was clearly thinking this would be enough to put Jules off. Instead, she marched straight to the front, took the stick insect from the zookeeper, and held it out on her palm. There was no chance she would have been that confident on her own. And she started to freak out a little as it headed up her wrist, but there was no way she was going to show Nate, or the children, that. Instead, she held it for what seemed like a reasonable amount of time, then handed it back to the zookeeper.

"Your turn, Mr Campbell."

It was unbelievably satisfying to see him squirm. His whole body was rigid, and the tension grew visibly tighter in his arms every time the creature moved. As he turned to give the animal back, Jules stepped forward, her phone out.

"Hold on one second. I think we should get a photo of you there." She took one snap, then moved to an angle to get another, each second Nate's glower on her intensifying as her look of pure joy rose. After a couple more, she turned back to the class. "Well, I think this looks perfect to go in this week's newsletter, don't you children?"

As they filtered out of the room, Nate sidled up beside her.

"You know, as weird as it is, somehow I like you even more now.'

CHAPTER 40

After the excitement of the education centre, the children started bickering for the first time all day. A sure sign that they needed to eat.

"Okay, time for food," Jules said, studying her map. "If my map reading skills are correct, then the adventure playground and picnic area are just over there." She pointed down a path. "Let's go."

The words "adventure playground" were all it took for the children to break out in a sprint.

"What did I say this morning?" Jules switched to her stern teacher's voice. This time it was even louder than at the rhino field but was just the right volume to make the children immediately slow. "Food first, then play," Jules said. Audible groans of disappointment rose around her. "And there's a tap there; please wash your hands before you eat."

One by one, the children took their seats on the picnic benches and started their food. For a second, Jules considered sitting with them, just so that she and Nate weren't alone, but she quickly changed her mind. If she had been grouped with any other parent or teacher, they would have sat on a neighbouring bench, close enough to watch all the children but far enough away that they didn't have to hear every word of their conversation.

"So what about if I go to the school? Say this is a thing," Nate said before Jules even took a seat, though she didn't quite understand what he was talking about.

"What do you mean?"

"You and me? What if I go to the school and ask the head's permission to date you? Is that something you can do?"

Jules let out a slight chuckle.

"I don't think so. Sounds like a Jane Austen novel gone wrong."

"What about next year, then? When Evie is not in your class anymore? Would that be better?"

Jules raised her eyebrows at the comment.

"Nate, that's ten months away. You're saying you're happy to put any form of relationship on hold for ten months for me?"

"Actually, it would be eight. That's when the term ends. Eight months isn't that bad."

A flicker of sadness sparked within her, but she couldn't respond. Nate shifted towards her and placed his hand flat on the picnic table. Jules stared at it. She would have liked nothing more than to place her own on top and intertwine their fingers, but that couldn't happen. Not here. And so she placed her hand, palm down, a little way from his. Their fingertips barely a centimetre apart.

"I don't want another relationship," Nate said softly. "I just want to be with you. Will you think about it?"

Her heart hammered in her chest as if it was close to exploding. Could she say yes? It felt like she could, but what would happen in the eight months until then? They'd see each other at the school gate and pretend they weren't both thinking about the moment they could wrap their arms around one another?

"Miss, can we go and play now?"

The voice snapped Jules back into the moment as she hurriedly pulled her hand off the table and away from Nate's. Broadening her smile, she stood up and moved over to the children's tables. "Okay guys, great eating. If you're done, please put all your rubbish away and then you can go play. But you've only got fifteen minutes, then we will head out to see the reptiles."

As she said this, she looked to Dylan, whose face lit up so much it practically glowed.

Over the next five minutes, the children wolfed down their food before escaping to the playground. Jules stood there, watching them jump and swing and race one another. It was hard not to think about Austin. How quickly the time went. It felt like a lifetime away, but she knew that in the blink of an eye, these children would be off to secondary school, too.

"It's "when"." Nate said, appearing by her side to watch the children scramble over the cargo nets.

Jules turned to face him, concerned she had somehow missed half the conversation.

"What's when?" she asked.

"Us. It's not, "if" it's "when"." And if that means waiting until Evie has left secondary school, then that's what it's going to be. It's you for me. I knew it that first night at the bar. And I know it sitting here now. And I'm pretty sure you know it too. But if you're not ready, and it really can't happen, we'll just be friends. Or acquaintances, if that's all you can handle. I won't push it. I don't need to, because one day you and I will be together. I know it."

Jules could feel the heat prickling behind her eyes. As

ridiculous as it was, the most romantic thing ever said to her happened while supervising half a dozen children on a jungle gym. She looked down and swallowed back the tears that were filling her throat, only to catch sight of the time on her watch.

"We need to get going," she said, before raising her voice to a playground level and calling to the children. "Okay, guys, time to get moving. Guys! Come on. If we don't get round to everything, we won't have time to go to the gift shop." At the mention of the gift shop, several children leapt from where they were, despite the height. Next time, she would tell them to climb down.

"Okay, where are you all?" The children lined up in front of her, ready to go. Jules looked at them and frowned.

"Where's Dylan?"

The children shrugged, and with a slight twinge of annoyance, Jules scanned the playground. The school uniform was normally easy to spot, particularly with their bright red duffle coats on, but at that moment, Jules couldn't see him.

"Evie, please can you go and find him? Tell him he should be back here."

Evie nodded before running off.

The children nattered away while Jules continued to look at her watch. Running a primary school trip, she often thought, was like a military operation, except people in the military normally listened to instructions. They'd be cutting the gift shop short at this rate.

A minute later, Evie raced back.

"He's not here, Miss," Evie said.

"What? What do you mean?"

"He's gone. I checked everywhere. He's not in the playground or the bathroom."

"Are you sure?"

"Positive. I shouted outside the boys' toilets. He would have heard. I was going to ask someone to check, but I didn't want to speak to a stranger. So shouting was the right thing to do, wasn't it?"

Evie's eyes were looking up at Jules, awaiting a response, but she didn't have one. Jules wasn't listening anymore. Dylan was gone. She had lost a student.

CHAPTER 41

The children's light chatter morphed into an outright cacophony, which was remarkably loud considering there were only seven of them remaining.

"He's been kidnapped!"

"He's been taken by aliens."

"No, he's just gone to the toilet, that's all," Jules interjected, stepping forward and quieting the children with her hands as she did so. "It's my mistake. I forgot he asked me to go."

"I thought Evie said—"

"There are lots of toilets in the zoo, Harri. I'm sure he just got confused about which to head to. Now, you can all just wait here and talk to each other for a second while I talk to Mr Campbell."

No matter how easily the children had bought the lie about Dylan being in the toilet, a glance at Nate told her he had seen straight through it. With a hand on her shoulder, he guided her slightly away from the students and lowered his voice.

"He didn't ask to go to the toilet, did he?"

"No." She took a staggering breath in, trying to conquer

the nausea that was rolling through her. She had lost a child. Of all the horrendous things to do, how could she have done this? How? She needed to think straight. To put a plan into action, but it was hard to concentrate on anything other than the overwhelming feeling of sickness. Especially with seven other children just out of earshot.

"He can't have gone far," Nate reasoned. "He was sitting with us when we had lunch."

"I watched him, watched them on the slide, and then… I should've been watching. I should've been watching him."

"Listen, you don't need to panic about this," Nate was holding her arms now. Comforting her. Or at least trying to. "Think logically. Where would he have gone?"

The moment Nate spoke, Jules realised the obvious. Of course, there was only one place Dylan would've gone.

"The reptile house!"

The slightest trace of a smile flickered on Nate's lips. "You go, see if he's there. I'll run some games with the children."

"You're sure?" The last thing she wanted to do was lose more of her students. But this was Nate. She trusted him.

"Go."

Jules's heart hammered in her chest as she sprinted down the pathway.

"Please, Dylan, please be with the snakes," she muttered to herself as she dashed through the zoo. "Please, just be with the snakes."

The reptile house was dark and dingy. As a child, it had been her least favourite place to visit in the zoo, and that hadn't changed as she'd become an adult. After all, a lot of the snakes looked pretty sneaky. A glass cabinet hardly felt enough to keep them trapped.

"Dylan! Dylan!" she called, nearly colliding with a family pushing a pram as she weaved through the crowd.

"I'm sorry. I'm sorry," she muttered. "I'm just looking for a child with a red— Dylan."

She would've recognised the St Catherine's duffel coat anywhere. There, with his nose pressed against the glass of the Burmese python's house, was Dylan.

"Dylan Searles. What on earth do you think you're doing?"

The small boy turned around, his chubby cheeks turning a dark shade of red. "Miss?"

"Do you have any idea how worried we were?"

"You said you were going to come to the reptile house first. I thought I could just wait here and meet you."

Jules's body was in a state of flux. The relief and fury – both at herself and Dylan – had her hands shaking at her side.

"Dylan, this is not acceptable. We have been worried out of our minds."

"But you should have known this was where I would be."

Jules gritted her teeth. "We need to get back to the others. After that stunt, you're lucky we're coming to the reptile house at all."

When she returned to the playground, her pulse had lowered only slightly while Nate had the group playing a game of Duck, Duck, Goose.

"Right, children, we've only got an hour left, and it's going to take us at least twenty minutes to get to the bus, which means we get fifteen minutes in the reptile house before we walk over to the gift shop."

The mention of the gift shop triggered applause from most of the children, except Dylan, who looked exceptionally surly.

"Only fifteen minutes with the snakes? What about my talk?"

Jules shot him a look that told him it was better if he stopped talking immediately.

When she reached the reptile house for the second time in

five minutes, Jules let the children go forward, with Dylan taking the lead in describing the various species and typical habitats to them.

"Are you okay?" Nate slid beside her, and momentarily slipped his hand into hers. After one tight squeeze, he dropped it. As good as it felt, she wished she could have held onto it for longer.

"Not really," she admitted, still suffering from the adrenaline drop. "That was ridiculous of me. How could I have lost sight of him?"

"It was hardly deliberate. He ran off. He's a kid. That's what they do."

"Not when they're under my care they don't. I'm going to have to report it. God knows what that's going to do to my chances of promotion next year."

Nate turned to face her.

"The child wandered off and went to the reptile house. You found him within three minutes. That hardly seems like something you have to report."

"It was three minutes too long." Jules shook her head and sighed. "If I don't say something, he'll probably go home and tell his mum how he was on his own for an hour and a half. Then I'll be in even more trouble." Nate didn't argue with that.

"I'm sorry. I feel like I'm to blame for this."

"Because you're so irresistible I couldn't take my eyes off you to look at the children?"

"Maybe," he smirked.

"No, this is on me. All me. Now, let's listen to Dylan's snake facts, because I'm almost certain I heard him tell the others he's giving us all a quiz on this on the way home.'

CHAPTER 42

The chatter had quietened down substantially on the return journey. The excitement of the morning replaced with tiredness. They would likely sleep well that evening. But while the children were looking forward to getting home and seeing their parents, Jules was dreading it. She would just tell the truth. That was all she could do. Tell the truth and apologise.

Back at school, as the children filtered off the bus. Jules headed straight for Dylan's parents. Rather than his mother, who dropped him off, it was his father who was collecting him.

"Mr Searles, may I have a word?"

Mr Searles ruffled the hair on his son's head before looking up and addressing Jules.

"A word? Of course."

Jules's eyes flickered momentarily to Dylan. It was only the most minuscule movement, but the father saw it, and knew exactly what it meant.

"Dylan mate, why don't you stand by the car? I'll just be a

minute." At his father's instructions, Dylan left them, although rather than heading to the car, he raced to join his friends. "Hope he had a good day. He was ever so excited today. Couldn't wait to see the snakes. Bloody snake crazy, that boy."

"About that." Jules picked her words as carefully as she could. She had run over what she was going to say at least a dozen times in her head on the way back, just to make sure she didn't say anything wrong. "There was a slight incident today. The children were given some free time to run about on the play area after they finished their lunch. Unfortunately, Dylan used that moment to slip away and head to the reptile house. He planned on waiting there until the rest of us joined him. Obviously, the moment I realised he was gone, I fetched him."

Mr Searles's cheeks drew inwards.

"What do you mean, he slipped away? Was he being supervised? Which teacher was in charge of watching him?"

"I can assure you he was being supervised. I was the teacher in charge of his group. I'm very sorry. Like I said, he was only gone for a matter of minutes."

"You let my child run off, in a zoo, full of strangers?"

Jules shifted her position slowly, aware that several parents were watching, eavesdropping, their attention drawn by Mr Searles's raised voice.

"I gave the children very clear instructions, Mr Searles. They were told that they were to remain in the play park area until we headed to the reptile house. It was Dylan—"

"You are going to blame my son for your lack of competence?"

Jules felt the sting.

"Mr Searles, I'm ever so sorry that this happened. I can assure you Dylan is completely fine."

"And you think I'm just going to take your word for it? I

need to speak to Mrs Dowling. You shouldn't be teaching here if you can't control the children."

It felt like the floor was slipping out beneath Jules. Everything that Mr Searles had said was right, of course. Jules should've been paying better attention to what was going on. But as Mr Searles pivoted, he found his path blocked.

"Sorry to interrupt. I just heard what you were saying to Miss Chard."

"Nate, this really isn't necessary." Jules's voice was low and almost trembling.

"I'm sorry, Miss Chard, but, I think it is. You did absolutely nothing wrong."

"I'm sorry, do I know who you are?" Mr Searles was a stocky man, with broad shoulders, and nearly a foot shorter than Nate, but as he pushed those shoulders back, he seemed to grow exponentially.

"Nate Campbell. My daughter, Evie, is in your son's class. I was the parent supervising Dylan's group with Miss Chard today."

Mr Searles's glare was frosty. "Then I shall mention your name to Mrs Dowling, too."

"Please, feel free to. I'll go afterwards, mentioning how the children were given very, very clear guidelines to follow. Your son deliberately took a moment when he knew Miss Chard wasn't looking at him to run away from the group."

"What are you saying?"

"I'm saying that this is not a case of negligence. This is just a case of a child behaving like some children do."

"How dare you?"

"I'm only saying what I saw. Children misbehave," said Nate.

"This isn't necessary, Mr Campbell, please." She placed a hand on his shoulder, hoping the gesture might be enough to stop him from saying any more, but he continued all the same. "Quite frankly, Mr Searles, you should be the one apologising to Miss Chard, and having a word with your son."

"So you're telling me how to parent now?"

"I'm just saying..."

Jules saw it happening in slow motion. But before she could step in between them, she saw the fist flying through the air.

"Nate!" she said, just as he fell to the ground.

CHAPTER 43

"How's it feeling now?" Jules said as she held the ice pack against Nate's cheekbone. The children she taught rarely resorted to fisticuffs, particularly not at a school like hers, and the ice packs were more commonly used for grazed knees or bumped elbows. Still, she was grateful they were there.

"I'm so sorry, Jules. I shouldn't have got involved." Nate winced.

"I'm not gonna lie. I don't think you made the situation any better."

"But the things he said to you…" Nate shook his head with his jaw clenched. All the anger was still there, pumping through him. "You probably think I'm a terrible person. Would you believe me if I said I've never got into a fight before?"

"I don't think that counts as getting into a fight, anyway. He was the one who did the hitting."

Nate offered a short, sharp chuckle.

"Fair enough. What do you think? Does the rugged look make me even more attractive?"

Shaking her head, Jules lifted away the ice pack to examine beneath. The skin was already starting to purple in places, and likely it would spread. By tomorrow morning, she suspected he would be sporting a rather impressive black eye.

"You know, I don't think I've ever seen a fight before," Jules said. Certainly not one where a man came to defend me, she wanted to add. But she didn't. She was here, holding the ice pack to Nate's cheek on the school grounds. Losing Dylan would have been enough to get her into trouble. Now it seemed small fry compared to what had just happened. "You shouldn't have done it though," she carried on. "However hard it was to hear, Mr Searles was entitled to speak like that. He trusted me to look after his child. He was scared, more than anything. A couple of hours and he probably would have calmed down. But put yourself in his shoes. Imagine it was Evie who'd gone off and got lost when I was supposed to be looking after her."

"Evie would never deliberately disobey you."

"That might be the case, but it doesn't change matters."

They were sitting in Jules's classroom as they spoke. Among the various parents and staff, Frances had been outside when the fight took place, and now had taken Evie into the music room to give Jules and Nate some privacy and time to talk. They had watched as Mr Searles disappeared into Dawn's office with his own ice pack around his knuckles. Now all Jules could do was wait.

"You should take Evie home," she said. "She doesn't want to be hanging around here all day."

"I'm not going anywhere. I'll come to the meeting if you want. Get your side across."

"That's sweet of you, Nate, but really there's no need. To be honest, I think it's only likely to make things worse."

He nodded. His hands were resting on his knee and never had Jules felt a more overwhelming urge to reach out and take one. After all, she didn't know how it could make matters worse. Her fingertips twitched as she shifted her hand slightly, only for a knock on the door to make her jump.

There, standing in the doorway, was Gethin, who looked from Jules to Nate and back again.

"Dawn is free to see you now, Miss Chard."

Wordlessly, she stood up, only to glance at Nate and shake her head. She didn't need him to come with her. This was all her doing.

As they walked towards the office, Gethin remained uncharacteristically silent. Perhaps he'd already spoken to the head and knew what the outcome of the situation was to be. Perhaps he already knew she was going to get fired.

"Are you coming in too?" she said when they reached the headteacher's office door. Gethin shook his head.

"I'll be around afterwards though, if you want to talk."

Jules swallowed, took a deep breath in and knocked against the door. A voice came from within.

"Come in."

With her heart in her throat, Jules stepped into the room, closing the door behind her before turning to face the headteacher.

"So," Dawn said. "It seems to have been a very eventful day.'

CHAPTER 44

Jules had been in the headteacher's office several times. It was where they came for their annual review, which, while sounding scary, was really just a chat, where Dawn told her how well she was doing. Jules had also come in to talk to the head about students, too. Concerns she was having, ones who were excelling or needing extra support. Very normal teacher things.

But she had never been in here because she was in trouble before. And she very much felt in trouble.

"Mr Searles is exceptionally upset." The way the headteacher started the conversation made Jules's nerves kick up even further. "Now, what I gather from him is that his child was lost and unsupervised at the zoo for quite some time. Is that correct?"

Jules took a deep breath. She'd already planned how she was going to explain the situation to the head, but that was before there had been a brawl in the playground, and when she'd assumed that Mr Searles would have been slightly more understanding.

"Dylan slipped away while they were all playing in the adventure playground. When I realised he wasn't there, I went to the reptile house. I knew that was where he would've gone. I found him straight away."

"So, how long are we talking about here?"

"A couple of minutes. He was just inside the reptile house when I reached him. It was a minute or so at most." Dawn nodded, and a silence swelled, which Jules broke immediately. "I know Mr Searles was upset, but honestly, I found Dylan straight away. Mr Campbell was there the whole time. He'll be able to corroborate that."

"Yes, I was going to come to Mr Campbell in a little bit."

The headteacher paused; the ensuing silence lengthened and spread throughout the room like quicksand. Never had Jules been more desperate to break the silence, but she didn't know what else she could say. She had spoken the truth. If that weren't enough, she didn't know what else she could do.

"Jules, I have a deep level of respect for you as a teacher," Dawn began again. The words struck Jules between the ribs. People always gave good news or a compliment before they gave bad news. It was a standard way to soften the blow. "Everybody in the school has the greatest respect for you. But we're not even two months into the term, and things don't seem quite up to your normal standard."

"Has one of the parents complained?" Horror flooded through her. No matter what was going on in her personal life, Jules always did her hardest to make sure it never leaked into the classroom. The thought of children being disappointed in their lessons was almost, if not more, heartbreaking than anything else that had gone on that day.

"No, no. In terms of the classroom, the parents have had no complaints. By all accounts, the children are still loving your class. But the same can't be said for the staff. I believe there was an incident with you leaving the set painting early. Possibly misleading a staff member as to why you couldn't be there?"

A flash of anger struck Jules. The only way Dawn would've heard that was from Philippa. She knew there was a reason she had never trusted that teacher.

"I'm afraid I had some personal issues."

"But you were fine when you went to the shops with Mr Campbell? Is that correct?" Jules was struggling to swallow, her throat was now so dry, and the pounding behind her temples felt like she was the one who had been clobbered outside, not Nate. Only when Dawn spoke again did Jules realise she hadn't replied.

"Juliana, I want you to be honest with me. Is there something going on between you and Mr Campbell that I should know about?"

Tears welling in her eyes, Jules looked up. She could lie, but then, was she even sure what the truth was? They had held hands a couple of times. And kissed another couple. But all of that was in the past. Or the future, if she was to believe what Nate had said earlier about waiting for her.

"I have to say, when Mrs Campbell came to me, I dismissed her concerns as nothing more than an upset ex-wife—"

"Flick came to see you?" The floor was slipping away beneath Jules as she dreaded to imagine what Flick had said.

"But I think the fact that he took a punch for you probably says all I need to know. Still, I would like to hear the situation from you."

Jules took a deep breath in. What was that saying about the truth setting you free? For some reason, she didn't quite believe it in this case. But she couldn't lie. Not when her job could very well be on the line.

"We met in the summer holidays," she began, "before I

knew he was Evie's father. Before I even knew Evie was in my class. When I discovered who he was, I stopped the relationship from developing further. It's never been..." How did she word this without saying *sexual* to her boss? "...physical," she chose.

Dawn nodded. "So, you haven't seen him on a personal level since you stopped the relationship?"

Tension gripped Jules's shoulders and neck. "He runs the sailing school my son is now part of. So, we have bumped into each other."

"But in a social situation?"

The headteacher's eyes were boring straight into her. Why was it so difficult to lie?

"Only as friends," she said. "I saw him straight after I learned about Evie. I met him to say nothing else could happen between us."

Dawn's chin dipped into a nod.

"There is a lot to take in right now, not least Mr Searles. Do you know if Mr Campbell is planning on pressing charges?"

"I... I wouldn't think so."

She nodded again, tight and contemplative and not really saying much at all.

"Fine, well, I have some thinking to do. This is not an easy situation. In terms of Dylan, I wish you had contacted me so we could have stopped the escalation. Then it may never have come to all this. But for now, I suggest you go home. We'll talk again on Monday.'

CHAPTER 45

Evie waited in the car while Jules and Nate spoke outside.

"How did it go?" Nate asked. "Are you in trouble?"

Jules shrugged. "She said she wants to sleep on it. We'll talk after the weekend."

"I'll email her. Ring her." He sounded so desperate, Jules wanted to hug him. But she definitely couldn't. Not now.

"Don't. Don't do that. It will only make things worse. She knows about you and me."

"How?" A deep frown line formed between his brows.

"To start with, Flick. She cornered me the other day. I didn't want to tell you. Well, turns out she went to Dawn too."

Nate's face flushed red. "What the hell? When I—"

"No," Jules reached out and touched his arm. "It wasn't just that. In fact, Dawn didn't believe her. She thought she was just paranoid. But when you took the punch… God, I could lose my job over this."

She hung her head, and this time it was Nate who rested his hand on her shoulders.

"You are not losing your job over this. I will take the school to court if it comes to that. It would be an unfair dismissal. I will get the best legal team there is."

She couldn't help but laugh, though the sound was laden with sadness.

"Nate, if I could take your hand right now I would. I hope you know that."

He tilted his head to the side as he studied her.

"Why do I feel like I'm not gonna like whatever it is you say next?"

Jules's breath quivered in her lungs as she forced herself to keep breathing.

"We need time apart. Proper time. The text messages, telephone calls. They need to stop. And I don't want you volunteering for anything at the school, not for this year at least."

"Jules, I think you are—"

"Believe me, if there was another way, I would take it. But maybe, maybe if I can show Dawn that this thing between you and me, whatever it was, is over now, then maybe that will be enough. I'm not likely to get any promotions in the foreseeable future, but at least I get to keep my job."

Nate reached out.

"Jules?"

"Please don't ring me. I mean it. I'll end up blocking your number and I don't think I can face that."

"There's really no other option?"

"You said you'd wait for me until she left school, right?"

"I will. I really will."

THE BOOK CLUB messaging group was going wild that evening. A book they'd read last year was being made into a movie, and they'd just learned who had been cast as the lead roles. Everyone had an opinion. She didn't care. Her heart hurt too much to think about fiction. In seventy-two hours she could be jobless, lodgerless and without Nate. She'd hit lows before, but never like this.

In the morning, when Austin came into her bedroom at eight, he was less than impressed to find Jules still asleep under the duvet.

"Mum, what are you doing? It's your day to take us to sailing. We need to pick James up in fifteen minutes?"

"You can take the bus again, can't you? There and back."

The news would have normally made Austin pleased, but instead he took a seat at the end of her bed. "Mum, are you okay? You didn't really speak at all last night. And you don't look too great now. Is it another bug or something? Maybe you need to go to the doctor's?"

"Nothing a day in bed won't sort out." She forced herself to smile.

"Do you want me to make you a cup of tea before I go? I think we've got some painkillers, if you need those?"

The heaviness in her heart deepened further.

"You know I am so lucky to have you," she said. "I don't know what I'd do without you."

"Possibly never get dressed on the weekend."

"There's a good chance that's true."

He laughed.

When Austin left fifteen minutes later, Jules couldn't bring herself to leave her bed. She picked up a book and tried to lose herself in the pages, but it was a romance. Every sweet word the man said made her think of Nate, and everything that pulled the two protagonists apart made her think of the two of them. She put the book down and instead picked up her phone and turned to her work emails. She had stayed up late, constantly checking, wondering if perhaps Dawn might email to let her know what the consequences of the Dylan incident would be. It was hard to know whether no correspondence was good news or bad news. Did it mean Dawn was going to let her off with a warning, perhaps a written one, but not take it any further than that? Or did it simply mean that she didn't want to ruin her weekend completely and would tell her that her job was on the line come Monday morning?

CHAPTER 46

Jules's stomach was in knots. Monday morning had rolled around. She hadn't received an email or telephone call from Dawn, but she was certain that something would have to happen soon. So, when she walked into the Monday morning briefing, her knees and hands were trembling.

"You okay?" Frances said as she took a seat next to her. "I messaged you over the weekend. You didn't reply."

"Sorry, I wasn't in a great place." It was an understatement. When Austin had returned home from sailing, he found Jules still in her pyjamas, yet even that hadn't been enough for her to get dressed. Sunday, she decided, was also going to be a pyjama day, meaning that Monday morning was the first time she'd had a shower in three days. And maybe it would have made her feel better, had it not also been the day when she would almost certainly hear from Dawn.

"And now?" Frances asked. "How are you feeling now?"

"Honestly? I have no idea."

It was a weak answer, but it was true. Terrified, sad, impatient. She had a thesaurus's worth of adjectives that could be used to describe her current state of mind, yet none of them seemed enough for the moment. Exhausted. She was definitely exhausted.

Jules was about to say as much when the double door at the front of the staff room opened and the management team rolled in. First Gethin, then Amanda ready to take her notes, then last, at the back, Dawn.

Jules sat up straight, fixing her attention on the head. "I just want to get this over and done with," she whispered to Frances. "Whatever's going to happen, it's the waiting that's killing me."

"I've got several notices to give." Dawn cleared her throat before she continued. "As it is assessment week this week, please remember not to give the children any homework, other than spellings and times tables. Also, we are holding the school science fair in three weeks, and some parents are a little stressed about their child's project. Keep in mind that the science projects are not to involve flames or acids. I've had some quite upset parents on the emails this weekend. And metal cannot go in microwaves. It's a good idea to reinforce that point too, after the incident with Prim Cole last year."

With the mention of parents and an incident, Jules was certain she would at least get a glance from Dawn, but the headteacher seemed to be looking anywhere other than her. And she still wasn't done.

"Obviously, the assembly went wonderfully well last Thursday and thank you to everyone who was involved in the zoo trip. That's all I've got for now but keep an eye on your emails and have a fantastic week."

With that, she turned and left. The chatter immediately rose among the rest of the staff as they stood up in their seats and began to walk out of the staffroom towards classrooms.

Jules, however, remained exactly where she was, too confused to move.

"Are you okay?" Frances asked.

"Not really." With a breath in, Jules dropped her head onto her knees. The fact that Dawn hadn't even made eye contact made Jules more certain that whatever news was about to come, it wasn't going to be good.

CHAPTER 47

With a hurricane of butterflies in her stomach, Jules got to her class. She never got nervous with her class normally, but this wasn't normal. This was a mess.

"Come on in, everyone," she said, opening the door and letting the children file in one by one.

Evie and Max were at the front of the queue, although Jules's eyes immediately went to where Dylan was standing, his gaze fixed on the floor.

"Sorry about running off on Friday, Miss," he muttered under his breath when he reached her. "I shouldn't have done that. And I'm really sorry about my dad's temper too. My mum told him off loads. She's made him go and speak to a counsellor now. He's going to stop him from getting angry."

Jules crouched down to her student's level. A wave of warmth flooded through her. "Thank you for the apology for running off. I appreciate that. But you don't need to apologise for your father. Those were his actions, not yours. Now go on and sit down."

A twist of guilt and sympathy rippled through Jules.

It was so strange. From the outside, all these families with the expensive cars and designer handbags looked like they had their lives sorted. Perhaps nobody had everything in their life quite as together as they appeared.

When all the class was seated on the mat, she began.

"Today we are going to be looking at the Great Fire of London. Now, does anybody know when this happened?"

Jules got through the day like it was normal, but it didn't feel right. She was detached. It was almost impossible not to get up and check her emails constantly. Why the hell hadn't Dawn sent her an email yet? It just didn't make any sense. Dawn had had the weekend to sleep on it. Now Jules needed to know where she stood. At lunch time she considered knocking on Dawn's door and demanding an answer, although she knew that was something she'd never be able to do. Besides, if the head was on the edge of a decision, an action like that might be just what she needed to push her into it and it might go the wrong way for Jules.

When the bell rang at three-thirty, Jules ushered her children out of the classroom, then headed straight to Frances.

"Why hasn't she said anything?" she said, sitting on one of the small tables. "She said she was going to speak to me after the weekend. Do you think I should message her? Do you think she's forgotten?"

"Forgotten that you lost a kid, or that your boyfriend got punched by another parent outside the school?" Frances grinned.

Jules scowled back.

"He's not my boyfriend. He's not my anything."

"Really, that's a shame. I wouldn't have gone into bat for you if I hadn't thought it was real love."

Jules sat up straight, looking her friend in the eye.

"What do you mean, you went into bat for me? You spoke to Dawn? About me?"

Everybody knew that Frances had Dawn's ear when it came to the running of the school. In fact, Dawn probably wouldn't be half the head she was without Frances there to support her. But she'd never imagined Frances would do something like that.

"What did you say to her?"

"Well, it's actually more what I said about myself."

"That doesn't make any sense. What do you mean?"

Frances picked up several pieces of paper that were lying on the desk. Handwriting practice by the looks of things, although it was far neater than Jules could do even now, so why they were still practising in Year 6 was a mystery to her. Still, her friend remained conspicuously silent.

"Frances? What did you say? What did you say to Dawn?"

"This and that."

"What does that mean?"

Finally, Frances stopped.

"I simply said that you handled the Dylan situation extremely professionally. After all, you were the one who alerted the parents, which you could easily not have done, that the altercation between Mr Campbell and Mr Searles had nothing to do with you at all, and that it's not in any school rules that consensual relationships between parents and staff are not allowed."

"And that's all you said?"

"Near enough."

Her gaze avoided Jules's, just enough for Jules to know there was more.

"What does 'near enough' mean?"

Again Frances when back to rearranging papers. The exact same handwriting papers she had moved only moments before. "What does 'near enough' mean, Frances?" Jules repeated.

With a heavy sigh, Frances turned to face her while dropping onto her chair.

"I might have commented that I was possibly thinking about retiring. Seriously. Maybe even thinking about handing my notice in at half term, so that I'd be gone at Christmas."

Jules's eyes widened.

"You did not?"

"I might have. I might have also asked exactly how she planned on analysing statistics and completing the strategic development plans without me there. Once I'd said that, she seemed to think that you had handled the situation quite well."

Jules shook her head in disbelief.

"Have I got this right? Are you saying that you blackmailed the head by saying you would quit if I was punished?"

Frances crinkled her nose.

"I would say blackmail is a very strong word. I merely made suggestions that would be to the benefit to the school. Come on, you made a mistake. We all make mistakes. If people got punished or fired every time they screwed up, we'd have nobody in the workforce at all. Besides, you are one of the best teachers in this school and she bloody well knows it. There would be complaints by the dozens if she tried getting rid of you or reprimanding you for this."

Jules was grateful for the compliment, but she wasn't sure she believed it.

"And you didn't say anything about Nate and me?" Jules added, remembering that other minor factor Frances had mentioned.

"I merely said that if you were in a relationship, then it says a lot that he didn't escalate that fight. Most men would."

Jules thought about it momentarily, but Frances was still speaking.

"Look, I didn't see much of the guy, and I don't really know anything about him. But I saw the way he defended you. He had your back, one hundred percent. And I know you don't do relationships. You think it's gonna be you and Austin together forever on your own. But a guy who keeps coming back, even when you keep sending him away, a guy who stands up for you that way, not with drama, not for a scene, but just because it was the right thing to do, is exactly what you need. In my opinion, at least, but then, what do I know?"

CHAPTER 48

As fate would have it, an email from Dawn was waiting in Jules's inbox by the time she got back to her classroom, thanking her for the way she'd handled the situation and sympathising for her being at the centre of the parents' brawl. Had it been any other time, Jules probably would have felt elated by this and she certainly felt a small degree of relief, although it faded the moment she arrived home.

All around her house, from the kitchen and the staircase and even the bathroom, brown packing boxes were scattered on the floor.

"I thought you weren't heading off for another week?" Jules said when she found Vicky on her hands and knees in the garage, working out how to disassemble her exercise bike. "You said you were going to do your packing this weekend?"

"I know, but I didn't realise that another of the nurses at the hospital – on a different ward – is moving to the same place. They've booked a moving van, but she's said she's got a load of space that I can put my stuff in."

"Wow," Jules said, not sure how else she could reply.

"I know. It's all crazy fast." Vicky pulled out a screw, causing the wheel of the exercise bike to roll out in front of her. "Oh, and before I forget, a girl at the hospital spoke to me today about wanting to rent the room. I sent her your details. She should be a good fit. She's currently living with her family, is very quiet. And a slight science-fiction nerd, but I figured that could work with your book club?"

"Thank you. You really don't have to worry. I can get by."

"I know. Though it's not the money I'm worried about, and as I'm leaving soon, I feel like I can say my piece without you biting my head off."

"That doesn't sound good," Jules said, with a twinge of nerves. Standing up, Vicky rested her arm against the wall.

"Jules, I've known you for years. I like to think there aren't many people who know you as well as I do. And Nate is the first guy I've thought might just deserve you. So what if you've had a messy start? For some couples, that's the best thing. You get through a load of crap together and that's how you know it's going to work later down the line."

"Please, Vicky, please let this go." It was one thing hearing it from Frances. The last thing she needed was for Vicky to jump on the same bandwagon too. Particularly as neither of them actually knew Nate.

"I will, but think about it, will you? You could always bring him to my leaving party on Friday."

Vicky's leaving party was only four days away. If Jules hadn't felt bad enough, that just about topped the day off. One thing she knew, though, was that she wasn't going to be asking Nate to join her.

At six o'clock on Friday, Jules was standing by the front door, ready to go.

"You are not to play video games the entire time," she said to Austin. "And eat some fruit."

"First, there is no fruit in the house, and second, I have way too much homework to do to play computer games."

"Good," Jules said. "And don't wait up for me. You've got sailing tomorrow, remember?"

Austin offered a withering look, as if she was the child and he was the adult, though it had felt more and more like that recently.

"Mum, try to have a good night tonight, okay? You deserve it."

She bent over and ruffled his hair before kissing him on his forehead.

Of all the places Vicky could have chosen for her leaving do, she had somehow decided on the damn White Horse. The place was filled with memories of her and Nate, though, as Jules sped inside, she was so quickly accosted, she didn't have time to think about it for long.

"It's been forever since we've seen you!" Sophie squeezed her into a tight hug. "Why didn't you turn up to the book club yesterday? We were all worried."

"Sorry." Jules let out a sigh. "Just a lot going on at the minute."

"That'll be the reason you haven't replied to our messages, too?" Maria said sceptically as she took Sophie's place, pulling Jules in.

"Sorry, I'll be better soon, I promise." Keen to turn the conversation away from her, she gestured to the room. "I can't believe how many people have come to say goodbye to Vicky. I guess a lot of them are from the hospital. She has been there a while."

"Well, we better find somewhere to sit," Sophie said, nodding towards one of the few free tables. "It looks like more people are coming, and there's no way I'll be able to stand all night in these heels."

Jules shifted her gaze to the doorway. Sophie was right, more people were coming. The door was currently open and a familiar face was standing and staring straight at her. It wasn't one of Vicky's nursing friends, though. Nor was it one of the book club girls who had adopted Vicky as their own, despite how she mercilessly mocked them. No, it was Flick.

CHAPTER 49

Their eyes met across the room. The same room, ridiculously, where Jules had first laid eyes on Nate, when she thought he was single and fun and maybe an answer to a dream she didn't know she had. Now though… now he was just the source of the constant sadness and throbbing in her chest.

Jules wanted to look away, or perhaps blink and find that Flick had disappeared, but she strode – albeit slightly more tentatively than normal – across to her.

A small smile flickered at the corner of Flick's mouth.

"It looks like I chose the wrong place to come," she said. "Is it a private party? I didn't see a sign outside."

Considering Jules had expected her to turn straight around or offer her a snide comment the way she'd done before, she wasn't prepared for her question, which was, by all account, entirely pleasant.

She cleared her throat before she spoke. "It is, well, sort of. We haven't booked it or anything, but these people are here for my friend Vicky. She's moving to Glasgow."

"Glasgow, that's a change."

"I know."

Silence formed between the two of them. One that Jules didn't know how she was supposed to break. The last time she had spoken to this woman, she had stood there and fielded a load of abuse. The last thing she wanted to do was to cause a scene on Vicky's day.

"In that case, I should probably find somewhere else to have my glass of wine. I don't want to look like a gate crasher," Flick said.

Relief flooded through Jules, but it didn't last long. What was it about Flick that made her feel so guilty? It wasn't just the Nate thing, she thought. It always felt like there was something more. As she watched Flick turn to go, she thought about the time they had bumped into each other at the taproom, and the time when Flick had rushed over from the other side of the road when she saw Jules with Nate. Finally, Jules realised what it was.

Flick was lonely. All the fancy clothes, the big car, the attitude at school, and it didn't matter. At the end of the day, she was lonely. That was why she came to the smallest bar in town to have a drink by herself. The thought caused the pang of guilt to deepen.

"No one will mind if you stay for one," Jules called as Flick turned away from her. "Nobody here knows everybody, anyway. Stay."

She wasn't sure why she had said it, but the smile that rose to Flick's eyes was enough to lessen the guilt be a fraction.

"Thank you, and let me get you one, too. I owe you that."

Jules nodded and stood silently by Flick as ordered the drinks. When the bar poured the two drinks, Flick handed one to Jules.

Silence swelled between them.

"I'm sorry," Flick said. "What I said before, it was horrible. I shouldn't have attacked you like that."

"You were upset."

"I know, but that's not an excuse." She paused, and Jules wondered what she was meant to say. Only Flick wasn't done yet.

"I heard about him taking the punch from that man at school last week, and people said it was because he was being rude to you."

Jules's stomach twisted. Of course, she'd known it would spread around the school, but she hadn't considered the gossip getting back to Flick.

"It was an upsetting event, but he shouldn't have done that. Stepping in."

"No, he probably shouldn't have. That's just the kind of thing that Nate does." She paused again and pressed her lips together. Somehow Jules knew it wasn't her time to speak. Flick had more to say, and she wanted to give her the time to do that. She took a long sip of her wine before her gaze met Jules's.

"I don't know if you remember, but I told you once how Nate's spark had returned, and I thought it might have been because of here. Because of the fresh start. But that wasn't the case, was it? It was because of you. He'd already met you. That's why he responded so badly in the classroom when he saw you?"

The noise of the bar muted around them. All Jules could see was this woman staring at her, wide-eyed and waiting for an answer, and her own twisting guilt that corkscrewed within her.

"It wasn't anything, really. It was over before it started. And it certainly wasn't a relationship. But I want you to know that I didn't know he was married."

Flick chuckled sadly. "I think it's fair to say our marriage ended well before you were on the scene, though I might not have wanted to admit it."

She pressed her lips together so tightly they disappeared into a line, and she lowered her gaze so that it was lost in her wine. When she lifted it up, she looked straight at Jules again.

"It's hard to let go, you know. You're a mother, right? You get it. You build your life around this person, these people. You change to fit what they are, and the world they live in. And then at some point, you don't even recognise the person looking back at you from the mirror. I don't know you very well. Only what Evie and the other parents have told me, but no one has a bad word to say about you."

"I'm sure you can't have listened too well, then."

"Okay, there was the one thing about a missing child, but I've heard both sides of that too." Flick chuckled. It was a little forced, but it caused a smile to flicker on Jules's lips, however briefly. "Nate is one of the best people I know, and it's fair to say I haven't handled the situation very well at all. And that's because of me, but him a little bit too. I think neither of us were willing to accept how much we'd changed since we first met. You know, I think under different circumstances, had you met the old me, the not-bitter me, you and I could actually be friends."

"I think you might be right," Jules replied truthfully.

"I know when people get divorced they're meant to only want the worst for their spouse, and for a while I felt like that, but that's not who I want to be. He's the father of my child. He was my best friend for years, and that part of me – the part I want to be – wants him to be happy more than anything else. So if there is perhaps a chance that he makes you happy too, then maybe it's not too late."

Jules closed her eyes, and she tried to absorb everything

that Flick had just said. Nate's ex-wife was there in front of her, telling her they should give it a go? The same woman who had practically threatened her if she went anywhere near Nate. If that wasn't a bizarre turn, she didn't know what was.

Even when she opened her eyes, Jules didn't know what to say.

"You can tell me to mind my own business," Flick carried on, doing anything but. "Evie's with Nate tonight, but I'm picking her up in the morning, and I know he's heading out to Burnham-on-Crouch first thing to have a look at a boat. Maybe if you don't have plans, a walk around Burnham might be a nice way for you to spend your Saturday morning, too?"

Jules wanted to hug her. She wanted to squeeze her tight and tell her she was sorry about the situation. But they weren't there yet. So instead, she offered her a smile. Nothing forced. Nothing painful, just a smile, as she said,

"Can I get you another drink?"

CHAPTER 50

Jules could barely keep her hands on the steering wheel.

"You don't mind getting there a little early, do you?" she said to Austin and James in the back of the car. "It's just such a lovely morning. I thought I might head to Burnham for a change of scenery while you were at the sailing club."

"Something's going on with her. She's said it's a lovely morning four times already," Austin said. "And it's not even that nice. Though the wind will be good for sailing."

Jules looked at the clouds as she drove. It had been Martin's turn to take James and Austin sailing, but seeing as she was up and about so early, it seemed silly for her not to do it instead.

"I'm just worried the weather is going to change, and then it'll be winter and we won't be able to go out for nice long walks and then everything will be cold and we'll be stuck inside and—"

"It's okay, Mum, we get it. Yes, we can wait at the sailing

club and you can go for your long walk wherever it is you need to go."

That was one of the problems. Jules wasn't entirely sure where she needed to go on this walk. Burnham had numerous yacht clubs, not to mention a marina, and Flick hadn't given her any more information before she left Vicky's party. So Jules wanted to give herself as much chance as possible of bumping into Nate.

Soon she had dropped off the boys and was alone with her bouncing nerves and racing heart for the rest of the journey. She had decided to park at the far end of Burnham, where the first yacht club was, and walk along the seawall. Halfway along, as she hit the houseboats and the ice cream counters, she realised how ridiculous this was. She had already passed two yacht clubs and there was no sign of him. The marina was still another half-mile walk and there was the added issue that he was looking at a boat, meaning he was probably out on the water.

The best thing she could do was ring him. Act like a normal person. Still, the thought fell heavily on her heart. She turned around to head back to the car, only to see him there, elbows resting on the wall. With her breath held, she took two steps towards him.

"Nate?"

It was definitely him, with a takeaway coffee cup in his hand, and a purple bruise on his cheek, although it didn't look half as bad as she expected.

"Jules." Their eyes locked as her heart raced. She wanted to kiss him. No, she needed to. She needed to kiss him out in public and show him that she wanted this, the way he had shown her so many times before. Yet as she shifted her feet, Nate cleared his throat and looked to his side. Only then did

Jules notice the man standing there. “Angus, Jules Chard. My daughter’s teacher.”

“And friend,” Jules said and stretched out her hand to shake Angus’s. The old man with a potbelly and rounded glasses nodded furiously, causing his jowls to wobble.

“Teacher, eh? Fabulous profession. Fabulous.”

Nate was still looking straight at Jules, confusion etched on his face.

“So... Jules, what are you doing here?”

Jules swallowed hard. In all the practices she had done in her head, she had never thought about there being another person present when they spoke.

“Actually, I was hoping to bump into you.”

“You were?” His eyes widened.

“I was. If you’ve got some free time, that is. If not, it’s no bother.”

Silence blossomed, but as Nate started to speak, he was interrupted.

“I—”

“I think we’re about wrapped up here,” Angus said, his voice booming an octave lower than Nate’s. It was, Jules considered, a voice she would be able to hear far out at sea.

“I don’t want to feel like I’m interrupting you,” she said.

“You’re not. Nathaniel, chap, let me have a gander at the numbers and I will get back to you on Monday if you’re okay with that.”

“Sounds great.” The two men shook hands before Angus turned his attention to Jules. “Lovely to meet you,” he said. “Perhaps we’ll meet again.”

“That would be lovely.”

With one last nod to Nate, Angus turned and began to walk along the seawall.

Together, Jules and Nate watched the figure disappear. Neither of them spoke. Even when Angus turned the corner and was no longer in view, their eyes remained locked out in the distance, as if neither of them were willing to look at one another. Finally, it was Nate who cleared his throat.

"Is everything okay?"

"Yes." Jules looked straight at him. Her eyes were drawn to the mark on his cheek. She desperately wanted to put her hand up and brush against it, but instead, she tipped her head quizzically.

"Are you wearing foundation?" she said.

"Concealer, actually. Black eyes don't work well in my line of business."

A brief chuckle freed itself from Jules's throat, but it didn't last long. Why did it feel like she just run a bloody marathon? And the sweat that was beading on her hands was now close to dripping. Never could she remember feeling quite this nervous in her life.

"Nate, I spoke to Flick yesterday."

"You did?" His face hardened.

"I did. I ran into her at the pub, and it was totally bizarre. She said how she didn't like the person she'd become. How she hadn't always been that way."

A sad, wistful smile graced Nate's lips.

"It's true. She used to be one of the good ones. One of the best."

"I can tell." She paused. "She told me she wanted you to be happy. And that she thought being with me would do that. I think she was genuine about it."

At this, his eyebrow arched upward.

"So?"

His bluntness unnerved her. She wasn't exactly sure what

she was expecting his reaction to be, but then she hadn't actually told him why she was there yet. All she'd done was mentioned his ex-wife.

"Nate, I think I got things wrong."

"What do you mean? What did you get wrong?"

"Life, I think. Definitely us. I mean, I thought I couldn't do my job properly if you were in my life, but I can't do my job properly when I don't have you either. And I have constantly told myself all the reasons we shouldn't be together, but I keep forgetting the reasons we should be."

"Go on." He moved towards her.

"You're really gonna make me do this? You're really gonna make me beg and tell you how wonderful you are?"

"It is definitely tempting when you say it like that," he said, the smile curling upward on his lips. "Actually, I have a far better idea of how you can convince me you're serious."

"Yes, how's that?" she said, feeling her body lean involuntarily forward.

"You can kiss me."

"In public?"

"Yes." She moved towards him only to pause, with her head only inches from his.

"Only if you do something for me first?"

"This doesn't sound like the deal we made."

She stood up straight and backed away from him, so she could see the look on his face when he heard what she had to say.

"I sent an email last night. It might have been a little presumptuous."

"An email?"

She nodded.

"I hope you're free Monday morning. We have a meeting with the head, where we tell her about our relationship."

"We have a relationship?"

"If you want?"

The kiss that followed gave her all the answers she needed.

EPILOGUE

Jules was nervous. It had felt like such a good idea at the time, even though it was a bit of a spur-of-the-moment decision, born out of one too many cocktails.

She had been out with the book club girls, enjoying herself and telling them all about Nate moving in with her and Austin.

"I can't believe he's already been living with us for over a month. Austin and him get on like a house on fire, and Evie, well, Austin already sees her as a little sister."

"We are so happy for you," Maria said, enveloping her in a hug.

"Wedding bells soon?" Sophie added.

"We're not rushing anything," Jules said, skipping over how quickly they had gone from making their relationship official to moving in together. She was about to tell them about the gift Austin had bought Nate for his birthday when she spotted something, or rather someone, on the other side of the pub. Flick was sitting by herself with a glass of wine in hand.

The other girls' eyes followed Jules's, only for them all to fall silent.

"Great. Just who you don't want to see," Sophie said. Jules ignored the comment. Instead, another thought popped into her mind.

She looked away from Flick and leaned in to whisper to the girls.

"Do you guys mind if we invite her over to join us?" she said.

Every pair of eyes widened at her.

"Why would you want to do that?" Sophie said. "She was horrible to you. Worse than horrible."

In some ways, it was understandable that the girls still hadn't forgiven Flick. The way she had confronted Jules at the school performance had made her enemies for life. But for Jules, that was water under the bridge. After instigating Jules and Nate's reunion, Jules felt Flick had done more than enough to redeem herself. Beyond that, she had been trying her best to accept their relationship, accepting that Evie now had her own bedroom at Jules's house too, which she also referred to as home. Jules's life couldn't have fallen together more perfectly, yet seeing Flick on her own niggled at that perfect Happy Ever After.

She pushed back her chair and walked over to Flick's table.

"Do you want to come and join us? We're just having cocktails," Jules said.

Flick looked up from her table.

"Jules, I thought that was you. I was going to say hello, but I didn't want to interrupt your evening," Flick replied.

"You wouldn't be," Jules said. "Honestly. Why don't you come over? Sophie has already had a bottle of wine, but if you can survive her whingeing about her useless boyfriend, you'll be fine."

"Are you sure?"

Jules couldn't help but think of the first time she had seen Nate's ex-wife. How confident she had seemed. How together. Now she knew the truth. Flick was as messed up as the rest of them. She was just a damn good actress.

"You never know. You might have fun," Jules assured her.

Only as they talked did Jules realise how little she knew about the woman. For starters, Flick had a wicked sense of humour, dry and sharp. It was immediately obvious why Nate had fallen for her. She'd also had a fascinating range of jobs before she and Nate got married, although her passion lay with photography.

They had just opened the next bottle of wine when Flick asked the question that possibly could have come earlier.

"So, how do you all know each other? You don't all work at the school, do you? Did you grow up in Maldon?"

"No." Gemma shook her head. "Some of us did, but we're all in a book club. The Lonely Hearts Book Club."

Flick tilted her head questioningly. "The Lonely Hearts Book Club?"

"For single people who can't get their love life together, although with Fleur and Jules now sickeningly in love, they're skewing the title a bit."

"Sounds like I would fit in perfectly," Flick muttered sadly to herself. It was a throwaway comment, Jules could tell, but the thought stuck in her mind.

"Well, why don't you come then?"

"Sorry?" Flick looked up, confused.

"Why don't you come to the book club?" Jules clarified.

The girls exchanged glances, slightly worried that perhaps Jules had had one too many to drink, but Jules didn't care. This was the right thing to do. She could feel it. Still, Flick didn't reply, but sipped her drink and hastily changed the conversation.

It was only when the evening drew to a close that the pair spoke again.

"I had a lovely night tonight," Flick said. "Unexpectedly lovely."

"I'm glad, and I meant what I said. You should join the book club. I'd like it if you joined. I think it would be good for Evie to see us getting on, and I think it would be really good for you. The girls are amazing. You'd have yourself an instant group of friends to whine about men to."

"I really don't..." Flick began, but Jules could see the hesitance in her eyes. She could see that she wanted this.

"It's every other Thursday. I'll get your number from Nate and text you the book we're reading," Jules interrupted, settling the matter.

With a small smile, Flick reached out her arms and hugged Jules tightly.

Another perfect match for the Lonely Hearts Book Club, but just how will Flick get on in her search for love? Why not find out in Illusions of Love, the third book in the Lonely Hearts Book Club series.

NOTE FROM HANNAH

First off, thank you for taking the time to read **Lessons in Love**.

If you leave a review for **Lessons in Love** on Amazon, Goodreads, or even your own blog or social media, I would love to read it. You can email me the link at Hannah@hannahlynnauthor.com

Don't forget, you can stay up-to-date on upcoming releases and sales by joining my newsletter, following my social media pages or visiting my website www.hannahlynnauthor.com

ABOUT THE AUTHOR

Hannah Lynn is an award-winning novelist. Publishing her first book, *Amendments* – a dark, dystopian speculative fiction novel, in 2015, she has since gone on to write *The Afterlife of Walter Augustus* – a contemporary fiction novel with a supernatural twist – which won the 2018 Kindle Storyteller Award and Gold Medal for Best Adult Fiction Ebook at the IPPY Awards, as well as the delightfully funny and poignant *Peas and Carrots series.*

While she freely moves between genres, her novels are recognisable for their character driven stories and wonderfully vivid description.

Born in 1984, Hannah grew up in the Cotswolds, UK. After graduating from university, she spent ten years as a teacher of physics, first in the UK, then in Thailand, Malaysia, Austria and Jordan. It was during this time, inspired by the imaginations of the young people she taught, she began writing short stories for children, before moving on to adult fiction.

Nowadays you will most likely find her busy writing at home with her husband and daughter, surrounded by a clowder of cats.

ACKNOWLEDGMENTS

Massive thanks must go to Eleanor for her amazing skill in helping me get this book edited.

To the very talented Diane Meacham for this fabulous cover.

Thank you to all of my beta readers who take the time to read early drafts and offer valuable feedback.

To my eagle-eyed team of proofreaders, Kath, Ana and Lucy.

Lastly, thank you to every reader who takes the time to read or listen to my stories.

Printed in Great Britain
by Amazon

62064272R00153